# Praise for Catherine Texier's Books

## VICTORINE

"Romantic... Echoes of both *Madame Bovary* and Kate Chopin's *The Awakening* suffuse a nevertheless inventive and artfully composed delineation of a beguiling and complicated woman's arduous journey toward self-understanding. A subtly textured fourth novel." Texier's best yet. *Kirkus Review*

"Brilliant... The place itself is the seduction." *Bookforum*

"Mesmerizing,..." *Booklist*

"A spellbinding novel." *The Sunday Advocate*, Baton Rouge.

"Reminiscent both of *Madame Bovary* and Duras' *The Lover.*" *Publishers Weekly*

"Absorbing... The novelist's brilliance in evoking the quiet tensions of marriage and motherhood engender an immediate sympathy." *San Francisco Chronicle*

## BREAKUP – *The End of a Love Story*

"Breakup is one of the angriest and most honest books I have ever read. I found it, by turns, disturbing, exhilarating, mesmerizing, and always utterly impossible to put down." Anne Lamott, author of *Bird by Bird* and *Crooked Little Heart*

"Powerful – illegitimate ... as good as Elizabeth Smart's classic, *By Grand Central Station I sat Down and Wept...* as good as Nora Ephron's *Heartburn...* a work that stands as a definitive statement of love and loss in this age of therapy. [It deals] with exquisite personal pain, of a kind I'd thought women no longer felt... elegantly, poetically written." Fay Weldon, *The New York Observer*

Breakup is an achingly true and uncomfortably bare account of the pain that only love—long, fruitful, complicated love—can inflict. But the surprise in Texier's recollection is her generosity of spirit, her soul-mining attempts to understand and empathize with the man who is betraying her and to even imagine the position of the dreaded other woman. With direct, immediate prose, meted out like news bulletins from the frontline of heartbreak, Texier takes the story of a woman scorned and turns it into the memoir of a human triumphant— and delivers an unputdownable book at the same time." Elizabeth Wurtzel, author of *Prozac Nation* and *Bitch*

*PANIC BLOOD*

"A surprisingly good read… The novel generates a sort of hard-boiled cynicism." *The New York Times Book Review*
"Texier writes with the kind of restless energy which continually suggests the fluidity and danger of white-water rapids – it has the same cruel beauty of potential death hidden beneath the rushing flow of life. It is also a sexy book, with Eva's private sexuality promoted as an inevitable, unstoppable force to be relished, embraced and indulged. But ultimately, it is about the price of staying alive as a woman." *Time Out* (London)

"Texier is … an extremely talented writer. She has an astonishing visual imagination that animates every detail of the book: Eva, with her emerald-green bustier, black hair in a twisted bun, carmine mouth and black Bakelite bracelet, is unforgettable. Similarly, wild child Mimi with her "sugary, oily" curls. Texier has great taste and delicacy when writing about sex, and combines powerful pornography with impeccably stylish sensual allure." *New Statesman* and *Society* (London)

*LOVE ME TENDER*

"Extraordinary… An explicit look at sex and survival on the Lower East Side. [*Love Me Tender*] is full of powerful, sensuous language." *The New York Times Magazine*

"Somewhere between a Henry Miller fantasy and a William Burroughs nightmare… Texier's prose reads like a brilliant translation from the French." James Atlas, *Vanity Fair*

"*Love Me Tender* [is] a novel made up of equal parts Kerouac and Proust... The author is a restrained, even delicate writer with an unusual ability to delineate sensory impressions and psychological states with a few deft strokes." *The Village Voice*

"Catherine Texier has written a splendid, unsentimental, erotic and risky novel." *Details*

"Sexy... Poignant... At times even rough... *Love Me Tender* is a female story of New York City, but most of all this book is a personal song..." Kathy Acker

"I enjoyed every word... One of the may things about this book that is so great is that Ms. Texier... writes in such a way as to allow us to experience the struggle for love and the uselessness of living with out it." Hubert Selby, Jr.

"Both fascinating and frightening in its eroticism." Edmund Cardoni, *American Book Review*

Catherine Texier

# RUSSIAN LESSONS

Catherine Texier was born and raised in France and writes both in French and in English. She is the author of five previous novels, *Chloé l'Atlantique*, *Love Me Tender*, *Panic Blood*, *Victorine* and *Young Woman With a Bunch of Lilac*, and a memoir, *Breakup*. She is the recipient of a National Endowment for the Arts Award and two New York Foundation for the Arts Fellowships. Her novel *Victorine* won *ELLE Magazine*'s 2004 Readers' Prize Best Novel of the Year. Her short fiction and essays have been widely anthologized. She was the co-editor of the literary magazine *Between C & D*, and has written for *The New York Times*, *Newsday*, *Elle*, *Harper's Bazaar*, *Cosmopolitan*, *Marie Claire*, and *Nerve.com*. She lives in New York City.

www.catherinetexier.com

Other books by the author:

FICTION

*Chloé l'Atlantique*

*Love Me Tender*

*Panic Blood*

*Victorine*

*Young Woman with a Bunch of Lilac*

NONFICTION

*Breakup: The End of a Love Story*

# RUSSIAN LESSONS

## Catherine Texier

**RAW**MEASH

# RUSSIAN LESSONS

# 1

It was the way he looked at me.

His pale, gray gaze burnt with an intensity, a naked knowingness, that you wouldn't expect from this hunk of a guy who had the air of a marine, or an ex-convict—a bit louche. He was standing by the buffet table, towering a head above everyone else. It was in February, one year after my divorce from David. Lulu had just turned eight. And me, I was still in the blur and craze of post-divorce mania, let loose after a nineteen-year relationship, and trying to write a novel that constantly eluded me. I had come to the party on impulse, after Jack, the Columbia University student I had been having a fling with, had cancelled our plans for the evening at the last moment. It was a Carnival party in a French photographer's loft. There was a wall of windows overlooking the Empire State Building in tight close-up. All you had to do was screw your neck up and there it was, the needle piercing the yellow sky, so close you could almost stretch your arm and touch it. A Manhattan postcard. Everybody was turned out in silly get-ups—Roman toga, Marie Antoinette, Tarzan—except him and me. I was in neck-to-toe black, my downtown uniform. He was all in white, loose cotton pants and T-shirt, as if he had come straight out of a yoga class—unless it was his idea of a disguise.

Or else it was his Russian accent. Those rolled *r*'s, those *w*'s that slip into *v*'s are unmistakable.

"From Moscow." His pale eyes coolly ran up and down my low-cut, black silk top and high-heeled boots. With his blond buzz cut, his massive shoulders, his long, calloused fingers that brushed against mine when he brought me a glass of wine— "sorry, no vodka left" —he stood out in this artsy crowd. I asked him how he knew the photographer.

"At Chelsea Flea Market. Right below 26th Street. Many Russians. Ever been there?" He picked up a handful of peanuts and spilled them all at once in his mouth, looking me in the eyes.

"Yes."

"And you, how you know him?"

"Actually, I hardly know him. We have mutual friends. I am French too."

The hard mask of his face melted, making him look very young. His eyes lit up with glee.

"You are! Did you see that French movie about young barman and older woman?"

That was too uncanny! I knew exactly what movie he was talking about. *L'Ecole de la Chair. The School of Flesh.* I had seen it the week before at the Quad on East 13th Street with Jack. It was about an attractive, successful fashion designer in her forties who picks up a twenty-year-old, penniless barman/hustler. She relishes her sense of power and control as she pays him for his services. But when she falls in love with him and invites him to move in with her, the balance of power between them shifts, and he turns the tables on her.

The Russian shifted his weight from one leg to the other and looked at me with an amused expression, as though challenging me. I took a sip of wine and held his gaze.

"You often go to the movies?"

"No. But I like French movies. And I liked that it was about older woman and younger guy." He drained his glass and set it down, adding, "You're not twenty."

I repressed a smile at his bluntness. This was going to be fun. Certainly a lot more fun than Jack, who kept breaking off our dates. "No. You're right. And you, how old are you?"

"Thirty." He shot me another naked look. "I like older women."

"Why?"

"Because they are deeper, more interesting."

I couldn't tell whether it was a line or if he meant it. Both maybe. It was obvious I was older than him, although he may not have known by how much because people usually thought I was younger than my age, fifty-two. But he wanted to make sure I knew that he knew. His wide-set, pale eyes looked at me calmly, not giving anything away.

Or maybe it was the way we danced.

It was one of those classic, fast-paced rock n' rolls, a Chuck Berry or a Fats Domino. I was surprised how good a dancer he was. Hadn't rock n' roll been forbidden in the Soviet Union? But of course he was young enough to have been a teenager under perestroika. For all I knew Moscow had been flooded with American music after the Berlin wall came down. I knew little about where he came from, and all of it from the Western press, which, presumably, wasn't to be trusted. He guided me so confidently, my body just fell in step with him. Each time he slid his arms along mine, his muscles brushed against my skin like steel ropes. During the next dance, which was slow, I laced my hands around his neck and in response his sex pushed into my stomach, as stiff and unyielding as the muscles in his arms. He reminded me of those men who would press themselves against us, the girls on summer vacation from Paris, in the darkness of the Côte d'Azur nightclubs. We let them come close for the dance, like bringing a flame to the tip of a finger, then fled. This guy had trouble written all over him.

After the slow was over, I noticed the Russian by the wall of windows in heated discussion with a dark-haired woman, or perhaps it wasn't so heated, it was hard to tell from a distance. I lost sight of the woman and he returned to the edge of the dance floor. Without looking at him I went to get my coat and my bag. He waited for me by the door.

"Can I take you home?" he asked. I said no, my car was parked at the curb. But when he handed me his cell phone, I punched in my number, and he gave me his card, which was engraved in red, with a view of the Red Square and a silhouette of Saint Basil's Cathedral, with all its cupolas. Printed below were the words FROM RUSSIA WITH LOVE, a phone number, a P.O. Box number, and his name, Yuri P. In spite of his looks, he wasn't an ex-marine; he sold Russian souvenirs at crafts fairs and flea markets.

When I got home I tossed his card in the box where I kept the phone numbers of all the men I had met, dated, or slept with since the divorce—the tangible accumulation of cards and torn pieces of paper or scribbled napkins slowly filling up the hole left by David's absence–and went straight to sleep. Lulu was coming back the next day from David and his girlfriend's and I had to be rested to absorb the onslaught of her fiery energy, tossing about her backpack and weekend bag, her shoes and jacket, and ravenously demanding dinner. But I when I woke up the next morning, it was the image of the Russian that flickered at the edge of my mind, his pale eyes peering into mine and his smoky voice saying, "I like older women."

# 2

From my table by the window of the East Village diner where I've agreed to meet him, I watch the Russian cross the street. He's wearing a pair of jeans, a big black leather coat and a Kangol cap. The leather coat makes me think: *mafia*. A frisson of excitement runs up and down my spine. When he called me in the morning, a few days after the party, his voice was deep, softer than in person, the long Russian vowels caressing, as if we were already intimate. He was in New York for the day, he said, he had a present for me. Could we get together?

A present? Really? I was intrigued.

He pushes the door open and towers over me, apologizing for being late – he has taken the wrong subway line or gotten off at the wrong stop. Under his arm is a package wrapped in newspaper, which he carefully sets down on the table.

"What is it?"

"Open."

The newspaper is written in Cyrillic characters. I decipher the headline, something about Gazprom, the Russian oil giant, and unpack two bottles, tall and narrow, their excessively long necks giving them a swan-like grace.

"Is very good wine from Moldavia. Sweet. For dessert." He watches me expectantly. "You drink wine?"

"Yes, of course. French people drink wine."

He explains he had to run all over Brighton Beach looking for a bottle, because he only had one at home and he thought one wasn't enough.

"You'll think of me when you drink it."

"It's very sweet of you."

He puts his cap on the table and calls the waitress to place our orders: Rolling Rock for me, coffee for him. When my beer comes he picks up the bottle and studies it with a comical frown as if it was a Molotov cocktail about to explode.

"Try it."

He twists his lips in disgust. "Too light. I prefer Guinness." He pulls out a pack of Parliaments from his pocket, lights up, and pushes the pack toward me. This was just before the turn of the century, when you could smoke in public places, before a lot of things happened, when life was still wild and carefree in New York, when America was jubilant about having won the Cold War, before we impaled ourselves onto the Millenium. Underneath his coat that he's just removed, a loose grayish-green long-sleeved T-shirt in a silky material drapes around his wide shoulders and clings to his powerful chest. Averting my eyes, I slip a cigarette out of his pack, and he leans forward to light it. And then he tells me his story.

Five years ago he met an American woman in the streets of Moscow and impulsively followed her to New York on a tourist visa. He only had five dollars in his pocket and spoke just a few words of English. He had done two years in the Soviet Army and finished a couple of years of college, after competing nationally as a swimming champion. But economically things were just too harsh in Russia in the 90s, there was only the chaos of Yeltsin's perestroika, and America was looming, finally within reach. He jumped at the opportunity.

I watch him, mesmerized, as he upends four packets of sugar into his coffee, asks the waitress for three more and stirs them vigorously. Of course things went south with the woman. "She played games with me. Always push-pull. American women, they boss everybody around. They act like men." Anyway, he ended up on a North Carolina farm, milking cows for $3.50 an hour. "Coming from Moscow, I thought it was good money. Imagine that!" Farming was a disaster in other ways too. He couldn't get laid. Even the local "water buffaloes" wouldn't touch him with a ten-foot stick.

He looks at me over his cup of coffee to see my reaction to his attack on American women, and perhaps to gauge if I, too, play games with men. His eyes are shrewd, like those of a salesman who insists he's got nothing up his sleeve.

"I don't play games," he adds. "I'm honest." *Hooonest* with a long 'o'.

His own game is so obvious I burst into laughter. I glimpse his shoulders, sculpted under the T-shirt the color of his eyes. His sheer physical presence and provocative vulgarity are dangerously sexy, as if we have been transported into a dive bar in Odessa, the kind where drunk sailors grope cheap girls with meaty hands and topple them in the back room. Except we are in the East Village, a block from my home, and I can walk away any time I want.

"What? You don't believe me?"

I take my time puffing on my cigarette. "I don't know. I don't know you."

"What do you think makes someone sexy?" he presses on.

His eyes are a bit too narrow, his forehead low and stubborn. His wide cheekbones are cut like blades. He can go from plain to strikingly handsome in a swift shift of expression. There's something primitive and incandescent about him. Pure male power. With my eyes I follow the volute of smoke curling above my nose and pretend to ponder his question.

"Sexual confidence," I say.

He looks impressed.

"You're smart."

A wave swells in my stomach, threatening to crash and engulf me. I haven't felt such powerful, raw, sexual attraction since Hank, a German artist I met when I first came to New York. He had a similar insolent gaze that possessed me before he even laid a hand on me. I was twenty-one then. He was twenty years older than me. Now the age difference is the reverse.

"What?"

"Nothing. It's getting late. I have to go get my daughter at gymnastics practice." I push my chair back and slip on my coat. "Thanks for the wine."

He stands up and nods with polite deference. "Children always come first."

I cringe at the cliché.

Outside, a fine drizzle has started, a mist so vaporous

it feels like a gauze caress. I kiss him on both cheeks, like we do in Paris. His skin is damp. He holds me against him for a beat. A rush of electricity pulses between us, but the bottles clutched under my elbow hamper me, and I quickly pull away.

"I call you in few days," he says.

Night has fallen. Puddles reflect the street lamps in a kaleidoscope of red and yellow, the pavement shines. I run to catch the light.

In the evening, after dinner, my friend Alba stops by to pick up her daughter, Corina, a teammate of Ludivine's, who came over after rhythmic gymnastics practice. I offer to open one of Yuri's bottles. The deep purple wine, almost the color of grape juice, flows thick into our glasses, so sugary that when a drop spills along the neck of the bottle, it coagulates like syrup. The taste is so sweet and at the same time so surprisingly sharp we can only take a few sips before declaring the wine undrinkable. I stick the cork into the bottle and put it away at the back of the liquor cabinet, as if I were banishing Yuri to Siberia, never to hear from him again.

## 3

"Yuri the Russian guy!" His voice explodes into the receiver a couple of days later, just as I am opening the file for my novel. It's about a *café-concert* singer who goes to Saigon in 1902 for a tour of the French Asian colonies, and stays to become the mistress of the Governor of Indochina. After months of research, I have written a couple of chapters, but no matter which way I turn my sentences around, they fall flat. They have spilled too neatly out of my library research. The characters sound stiff and formal, like in a pastiche of a nineteenth-century novel. The book refuses to get up and dance.

As soon as I hear Yuri's voice I shut down my computer with relief, sensing some visceral incompatibility between his infectious liveliness and the words crawling on the screen.

"I want to have dinner in French restaurant," he says, disposing of any greetings. Not: How are you? Not: What's up? Not: Would you like to? No, just that: *I want*.

This *I want* gives me a pang. I swallow hard. But when I speculate where dinner would inevitably lead us afterwards, I dither. Still Yuri charges ahead full throttle. My instinct tells me, no, you're going to get in over your head. But why not? I am not twenty, as he said. I am free. The very idea of freedom is vertiginous.

"Are you there?"

"Yes."

"You pick restaurant."

"Where are you going, *maman*?" Her dinner finished, Ludivine has moved to the couch to watch TV with her babysitter. She glances at my jacket, the plum-colored gabardine one, cinched at the waist, and at my boots, the high-heeled, black ones.

"Dinner with friends," I answer with a neutral voice, hoping the plural will be good camouflage, but she isn't duped.

"Where are you meeting him?"

I feel my cheeks turn red at this "him," but before I have time to answer she turns her attention back to Rugrats, along with her babysitter who seems to be even more absorbed in the show than she is. Anyway, it's out of the question to mention Yuri to her. Whatever happens with him, she is off-limits.

* * *

"Did you drink my wine? What did you think of it?"

Still wearing his leather coat in the restaurant, Yuri leans forward, elbows on the table, eager to hear my verdict. I lie and tell him I liked it, but I found it a little sweet. Picking up on my shiftiness, he insists, "Have you finished the bottle?" I say, "No, not yet," feeling dishonest. *Dishooonest*. But when the waiter brings our menus, which read CHEZ PIERROT – BISTRO, Yuri gets all

24

excited.

"Bistro, you know it comes from Russian language? Bistro means quick. Bistro is restaurant where you can be served quick."

"*Znaio.*"

He looks astonished. "*Tyi govorish po-russki?*"

"*Nimnoshko.* I studied a long time ago at the university."

At that moment, the blues band at the back attacks the first measures of an old standard, which prompts Yuri to turn around with a dejected look and request a French song. The waiter looks at him blankly. Yuri repeats the question more forcefully. I can hear the strain in his voice, his expression suggesting that he would rather bang his fist on the table to obtain satisfaction. The waiter stiffens. I am mortified, beating myself up for accepting the dinner invitation.

"They don't do that here, Yuri," I say. Then I explain to the waiter, "He's from Russia."

The arrival of the bottle of wine saves us from terminal awkwardness. With curiosity, Yuri watches the waiter wipe the side of the bottle of wine before slipping it into the ice bucket. Thinking of the cloyingly sweet taste of the Moldavian wine, I am afraid the Sauvignon Blanc won't pass muster with him—my national pride is at stake, after all—but he nods approvingly after his first sip and, pushing the menu aside, asks for fish. The waiter recites the list of specials like a robot turned at top speed, looking at me only. Yuri, who hasn't understood a word, orders fish again with a sharper voice, trying to assert himself. The waiter, ignoring him, repeats his tirade. They are like two deaf people unable to communicate with each other. To break the tension, I choose the salmon special for him, and tortellini for me. But Yuri admonishes me as soon as the waiter is out of range, "Pasta is dish you eat at home, at restaurant you eat something better."

The young, very proper couple sitting at the next table furtively steal glances at us.

I am so annoyed by his reprimand, and so embarrassed, that I don't bother explaining that pasta can be a delicacy in France and in Italy. We eat in angry silence until he notices I am not finishing my food and he reaches over to clean up my plate.

"I thought pasta wasn't good enough to eat in a restaurant?"

"You should always finish plate."

"Jesus! You're so opinionated! You sound like my grandmother!"

"Russian people very opinionated." He comically moves his eyebrows up and down to make me laugh, but he's not even getting a smile out of me. "Is wrong?"

The young couple is now openly staring at us.

"No. It's just annoying. If you're done, I think we should go."

He looks at me for a moment, pushes his empty plate to the side and calls the waiter, who takes his time bringing the check, his face still a mask of disdain. Yuri drops eighty dollars in cash in the tray, adding, "Keep change," his only revenge the grand gesture of a big tip.

As soon as we are outside on the sidewalk, he uncoils his long limbs like a caged lion finally released out in the wild, the flaps of his big black leather coat fluttering in the wind, and suggests a "walk in park." Now that we are on our own in the street, my anger recedes, and I lead him through the dark streets of Alphabet City toward the East River Park. His determined, supple strides suggest that we might be on our way to a thrilling adventure in some dark jungle rather than to a mangy ribbon of green squeezed along the FDR Drive. We walk side by side in silence, so close I catch faint whiffs of sweat under his pungent aftershave. When we get to the promenade along the river, our hands touch each other by chance, triggering such a rush of electricity that I step aside and lean over the railing, pointing to the other bank of the East River.

"Look, it's Brooklyn, over there."

"I know."

In one quick move, without any warning, he takes me by the waist, lifts me up like a butterfly and deposits me on the edge of the parapet. I scream, terrified to tip over and be engulfed by the churning waters below, and give him a kick in the shin. But the feeling of his steely arms firmly roped around my waist makes my heart beat with excitement.

He laughs wildly, hyena style. "You don't trust me?"

"Let go! I have vertigo!"

He holds me for a while longer, just to make it clear that he's in charge, then loosens his grip and sets me free. I jump down and run away from him.

"You don't trust me," he repeats with a sad, slightly offended voice, catching up with me in two strides. "You should. You're safe with me." He takes my wrist. "Come on, was joke. Let's sit down and smoke cigarette."

A little out of breath, we sit on a bench and smoke. It's

past midnight. At this time the park is usually deserted, except for a few junkies roaming the north end. Yuri is wrong, I trust him. Enough, at least, to walk around the East River Park with him in the middle of the night, which I might not risk with an American man. He pulls a little plastic bottle of Poland Spring out of his pocket and offers me a sip. I almost spit it out. It's vodka. He laughs at my surprise. A pleasant warmth envelops me and I rest my head against the back of the bench.

"I want to be successful," he suddenly says, out of the blue, leaning his elbows on his knees. "I want to learn how to do it American way. You know Dale Carnegie? I am reading book. Willy Loman. You know who he is?"

"*Death of a Salesman*? Yeah." I fail to see the connection between Dale Carnegie and Willy Loman, but OK.

"You do? I want to be Willy Loman."

"It's a play by Arthur Miller, you know. A classic."

"I know," he replies, brushing aside my pedantic comment with a wave of his hand. "I want to be great salesman. The best of all." He exhales smoke with the determined breath of a man intent on carving his own fate, and smashes his half-consumed cigarette with an angry heel. Then, without transition, as if to seal his grandiose plans, he lifts my chin, peers into my eyes, then runs his hand over my breasts, down my stomach, and kisses me hard.

"I want you."

There's no tenderness in his kiss, only pure, carnal desire, tumbling me into a deep well, its dark water thick and icy, his hands already fumbling between my legs. Then he picks me up and straddles me on top of him, his erection powerfully grinding into me. But the mood is killed. Yuri as Willy Loman, carrying his sad little cardboard suitcase door to door, is just not as sexy as Yuri the wild sailor.

"Not here." I struggle to my feet. "I have to go. The babysitter's waiting for me."

This word, babysitter, works its ice-cold damper. We walk back in silence, apart from each other, as if the slightest touch of skin might set us off again, until we arrive at my building. I climb up a couple of steps on my stoop to reach Yuri's height and turn around to give him a goodbye kiss on the cheek. Instead, he points a nonchalant index finger towards the crotch of my skinny jeans, almost touching the little round space above the swelling of the thighs – thus regaining, in one fell swoop, the terrain he had lost.

"Very sexy."

Stunned by his boldness, I turn on my heels without saying anything and bang the door behind me.

## 4

"Don't forget my green-and-purple-hair Barbie and my Hollywood Barbie," Lulu orders from her perch on the couch armrest while I pack her bag for her weekend at David's. Meanwhile, Yuri has invited me to Brighton Beach. "We go running on beach. Weather beautiful in Brooklyn." As if we were going to the Hamptons or the Caribbean for an exotic getaway. Actually, it *is* exotic to me. I can see myself taking notes and turning the adventure into a fun little journalistic piece. "Weekend at Brighton Beach." Would that fly in the *New York Times* travel section? As I finish packing Lulu's bag, it occurs to me that, since David lives by the West Side Highway, I could swing into the Battery Park Tunnel after dropping her off and head straight to Brooklyn, but I feel compelled to separate the two trips. The mother cannot coexist with the lover. So I first drop Lulu off, then drive all the way back home, change into a slinky top and a pair of wedged espadrilles, pull my hair up in a loose bun and don a pair of oversize, movie star sunglasses. Before leaving, I call Alba, the only person who knows of Yuri's existence, and tell her I'm going to Little Odessa. "If you don't have news from me by Monday call the cops," I chuckle. She laughs and wishes me a good weekend.

The ocean, along the Belt Parkway, glitters in the cold sun. The maritime landscape always comes as a shock to me after leaving Manhattan's thick forest of buildings, as though it were inconceivable that nature could exist in such close proximity to concrete. Even with the sunglasses, my eyes have trouble adjusting to the blinding light. At first, the ocean evokes a field of snow, then, briefly, the Mediterranean coast along the *Autoroute du Soleil* going from Cannes to Nice. Then it turns into the Black Sea, and at each exit I pass—Coney Island, Kings Highway, and finally Brighton Beach—I substitute the names of port cities in Crimea: Sebastopol, Kerch, Yalta.

Yuri is waiting for me at the entrance to his building, elegantly dressed in a pair of brown slacks and lace-up shoes, and a long-sleeved tan polo shirt. Even his hair looks different, longer, more polished, slicked back. As we ride the elevator to the fifth floor, to the apartment he shares with a computer programmer from Minsk, I note that Yuri looks like a man I could even date in the conventional sense. One look at his bedroom dissolves my dating fantasy. Narrow bed covered with a sleeping-bag, table from which hangs a piece of blue felt, stacked with cardboard boxes up to the ceiling, TV perched high on a dresser, suitcases piled in a corner, bulging plastic bags dangerously strained, ready to topple and spill out their contents. It's the room of a transient. But when I walk up to the big picture window, the deserted beach looks like it has floated across several oceans and clamped itself to this bit of the Eastern Seaboard, giving me a thrilling feeling of displacement.

"You bring bathing suit?"

"No!" My eyes open in mock horror. "Too cold!"

He looks so disappointed I hurry to the bathroom to change into my gym clothes. When I come out he's changed too, into sweatpants, a T-shirt, and a windbreaker. We jog side by side like two comrades into the sun, which is already angling west, passing cement block and rock jetties. The brisk ocean air fills my lungs in great, exhilarating waves. After a while I raise my arm to let him know that he should run ahead of me. He climbs on a rock and moves his arms and legs erratically to make fun of my running style.

"Sure you don't want to swim?"

"No way! It's March. I hate cold water." Still, not wanting to pass for a sissy, I untie my sneakers, roll my pants up and run into the icy waves. He squeals with a little boy's delight when he notices my lavender toenails, then laughs ruefully.

"Is nothing. In Russia, we used to break ice in frozen sea and when we came out we drank vodka to warm up."

He's already stripped down to his bathing suit, a tight Speedo, and carefully folds up his clothes on the rock. His body looks much more at ease undressed than ensconced in street clothes. He dives in and swiftly moves to the open sea in fast, powerful strokes. I sit on the rock and slip his jacket on to keep warm, watching his head bob up and down, way out, like a buoy. Just when he swims back, a man walks by, wrapped in a parka and a scarf, and stares at him as he emerges out of the ocean. With his long legs, narrow hips, his wide shoulders and his arms covered with a pale down, Yuri looks like a fearless Norse God. He winks at me and leans over to pick up his towel that has fallen off the rock. Frowning, he shakes it to make sure all trace of sand has been abolished, and rubs his back and thighs. I imagine him as a husband, berating me for having neglected to keep an eye on the towel. But I am not his wife, and I watch him with an anthropologist's avid curiosity.

I offer him his jacket, but he refuses and throws the towel over his shoulder. "I've spent two years in Russian army. Is little rougher than this. I'd like to see those wimpy Americans, see if they could survive if there's war on US territory."

As I watch him walk tall and proud by my side in his thin T-shirt, his white skin slightly mottled with goose bumps, I wonder if the only way to withstand the immigrant's unavoidable humiliations is to convince yourself that you are more of a man than the Americans, who are spoiled by their easy life, like Roman soldiers lounging on Capri.

On the coffee table Yuri has laid out a tin of gleaming black caviar, a jar of butter, black bread, and a chilled bottle of vodka. He splashes blackcurrant juice in my shot glass and shows me how to drink it, bottoms up, head tilted back. The vodka shoots like molten lava down my stomach. Then he lathers a thick coat of butter and an even thicker coat of caviar on a piece of bread and delicately places it into my mouth.

"You like?"

"Yummm. Delicious."

We toast another shot of vodka, which I only sip,

this time, under Yuri's disapproving frown. He pops the cassette of the Russian singer whose poster hangs on the wall. His "hero." He writes down his name in Cyrillic letters on my notebook and I copy it awkwardly. Vusotsky.

"Thousand of people showed up for funeral when he died," he says somberly. "He was symbol of Russian soul and freedom."

Feeling bad for my ignorance, I close my eyes and listen to the music. When I reopen them, Yuri is carrying a teapot covered with a red and white dishcloth. In a certain angle, with the dishcloth over the teapot, the bread roughly sliced, the surf pounding outside the window, the singer's raucous voice, Yuri's little room could be that of a fisherman a hundred years ago.

The tea is strong and black, piping hot. Comforting.

He leans against the back of the couch, stretching his long legs under the table. "In Moscow, was crazy in the eighties, when everything was falling apart." He sighs, nostalgic over the memories: Pyramid schemes. Vodka lines under the snow. Wild parties, chasing girls around and pinning them against the wall. "I was so shy, I didn't know how to approach woman." Moonshine vodka. Bottlenecks crashed against the wall because they couldn't be bothered to unscrew them. Women's panties hanging from the chandeliers. Bullying and scabies in the army. The bike that he had rigged, and his accident, the engine exploding between his legs.

"Look."

He pulls up his pant legs and shows me the scar, which I hadn't noticed at the beach, a long suture of skin from a graft running down the inside of his thigh down to his knee.

These are violent, dark scenes. Set in Moscow, unhinged by perestroika, they take on a forbidding, almost medieval allure. The men I have dated since my divorce have mostly been younger versions of David, well educated with MFAs or MBAs. With his fierce presence, his street smarts, Yuri blows them all away.

"I bore you?" His eyes, unsure, search mine.

"No. Not at all."

On the contrary, I am riveted. He could go on and on. The more gruesome and graphic, the better. No wonder teenage girls are suckers for horror stories. Fear is a powerful aphrodisiac. He leans toward me and runs his hands over my breasts and down my stomach, like he had done on the bench of the East River Park, except this time I don't stop him. He gently presses my legs open, taking his time stroking them all the way down and then slowly coming back up. Like with that first shot of vodka, intense lines of fire flare up throughout my body everywhere his hands have been. He pops my pants open and slips his hand under my panties, all the time peering into my eyes, with the same watchful expression he had when I was tasting the caviar or when he asked me if I had liked his wine—as if I were the female of a strange species he had never encountered before.

His lips hover over mine, teasing me with the tip of his tongue, and he pulls back to watch me, his fingers probing deeper into me while I dissolve against him. Then he suddenly stands up, his sex sticking out of its nest of pale blond pubic hair, imperious. He whips out a condom, and, kneeling on either side of me, folding my legs against his chest, takes me straight up till I scream.

"You like if I'm rough?"

"Not too rough," I whisper.

"But a little, yes?"

There's a term, I vaguely remember, for the Russian cavalry sweeping down to fight the Tatar invaders and raping every girl in their path without losing a breath. Cossacks? Or is it Hussards? That's how it feels like, a storm ravaging me, tossing me upside down into a wild torrent, still half-dressed, my bra and tank top pushed up under my arms, my naked legs spread open around his hips, while he presses me to him in deep, hungry bursts.

"Let yourself go. Don't you know pleasure comes past pain, is like yoga." I rock under him, creased like an origami paper girl, pliable and docile, yielding to the sure hand of a master until I abandon all resistance. My moans are the signal he's been waiting for; a long, deep wave takes us over.

He lets the condom drop to the floor and slips a playful finger into me. "You were well fucked. That's how you should always be fucked."

And we both erupt into an enormous laugh that leaves us breathless.

The night has fallen on Brighton Beach. The big, rectangular window is framing the night sky and a sliver of a moon. A Pink Floyd video plays in a loop, a swirl of psychedelic shapes, in bizarre contrast to the medieval mood. I can't put the cultural signs together. It's like entering a Cubist painting. Nothing seems to fit. I am missing the key. Yuri pulls a cardboard box down from a

36

shelf and takes out a stack of photos.

"Look. My mother."

A black-and-white snapshot of a plain, young woman with a soft face, holding a little boy with curly hair in her arms. I recognize his pale eyes, his small chin. I watch avidly, as if the key to Yuri could be found in the sad eyes of the young woman, who seems to belong to another century, although she is probably about my age.

"She died when I was eleven."

"Really? What did she die of?"

He doesn't answer. "She was from Caucasus. I loved her. I could never love woman like I loved her."

I cross my legs and pull the blanket over my shoulders, touched and a little embarrassed. Is Yuri so lonely that he needs to open his life the first time he sleeps with a woman? He stretches on the sheet and leans his head on my lap. I run my palm over his hair.

"What happened to your long hair?"

"I cut short, otherwise it curls." He chuckles. "Like girl." He hands me two more photos. His father and his stepmother. His father looks a little like Slobodan Milosevic. His stepmother has short brown hair. Plain face too. No makeup. Blouse printed with tiny flowers, collar buttoned up to the neck.

When his mother died, he tells me, he moved in with his father and stepmother in Moscow. His father worked at night as a printer, and he and his stepmother were alone in the apartment. Through the glass door, when the curtain was not completely pulled he watched her get undressed. "I was voyeur already." He pauses and looks up at me, uncertain of my reaction. I say nothing. I just move a little

37

to shift the weight of his head on my legs.

"You shocked?"

"No."

"I've always been obsessed with sex. I watched mother getting undressed when I was two."

"You remember when you were two?"

"Yes. Very well."

We stay silent for a moment. Then, with a finger, he traces the top of my knee. "Wanna have sex?"

I nod.

He laughs. "You're like me. Sex-obsessed."

When I wake up in the gray light of a cloudy afternoon, my outstretched arm, palm open, seems detached from me, a limb abandoned on the twisted sheet. Yuri has cleared the table and put the food away. Squatting next to me, he pulls a plastic bag out of a box on the floor.

"You up? Here. I have something for you."

Miniature animals carved in a clear, gold-orange resin tumble into my hands. An elephant, a cat, a frog, a monkey, a dog—none bigger than a nail.

"Is amber. I sell them at fairs. Choose."

Yuri's offering reminds me of those small presents teenage Arab boys sometimes gave us when David and I were traveling in Morocco and Algeria: a tape of rai music, a silver Fatma hand, a wooden snake—to seal a friendship that we knew would not survive our departure from their town.

"Thanks." I pick up the frog because I am French, and instantly feel an urge to get back to my airy, pristine apartment with Lulu.

On the way out, we buy two cups of coffee on Ocean

Parkway and carry them to a bench facing the ocean. Women in fur coats and hats, and men in heavy overcoats stroll, arm in arm, on the boardwalk, looking like extras in a Soviet film.

"Does the shore here look anything like the Baltic Sea?" I ask. "Or like the Black Sea?"

He shrugs with indifference. "I don't know, but I want to buy house on Jersey shore one day. And Mercedes." He sets his cup of coffee on the bench between us and opens his hands a foot apart. "Extra-long one. You know which one?"

I shake my head.

"And then one day, maybe I get married and have kids. But first I have to get legal status. I know Russian woman. She has US citizenship. I pay her $6,000. I move in with her and get married so that I can have papers."

A green card and a family. The immigrant's dream. I remember how thrilled I was when I got my green card a year after marrying David, holding in my hands that little bit of laminated cardboard which turned out to be blue and not green, the symbol of my own American dream. I never thought of what would happen after the dream came true.

# 5

David is strolling out of a midtown building accompanied
by a group of film producers just as I am walking by. He
comes up to me with a seductive smile, slowly unbuttons
his pants and penetrates me, right on the sidewalk, in front
of the astounded producers. The dream gives me a fugitive
feeling of triumph, quickly dispelled by the crystalline
sounds of Ludivine's glass beads curtain, which encloses
her bed like an Arabian Nights alcove. She is standing at
my door, barefoot in the pitch-black, pre-dawn morning,
hairbrush and bottle of gel under her arm, her hands filled
with bobby pins.

"Mom, can you do my bun?"

Another rhythmic gymnastics competition morning.

On the way uptown, we pick up Corina, Lulu's
teammate, and speed up the deserted West Side Highway.
By the time we cross the George Washington Bridge, a pale
light is sponging out of the darkness. Behind me the girls are
dozing off, leaning against each other. Hopefully the buns
will survive the trip without damage. I turn the radio on to
a jazz station; a Miles Davis tune from Bitches Brew rises
between the steamed up windows, lulling the girls to sleep
until we pull up at the school where the meet is to take place.

The bathroom scene is always the same: diaphanous, little blond girls, mostly Russian, pursued by heavy-set mothers armed with hair brushes, hairpins sticking out between their teeth, attempting to achieve the *de rigueur* ballerina bun balanced on top of the head like a brioche. While I lather an extra coat of gel to Corina's and Lulu's buns, mothers and daughters volley interjections back and forth. But in spite of all my efforts, the only words I recognize are *spacibo* and *pozhalyusta* and *harosho*.

From my spot on the bench, I can see hoops peeking and multicolored ribbons slithering above the curtain that separates the auditorium from the warm-up area. Two or three mothers I know are scattered around the bleachers. We wave at one another and stand up for an atrocious rendering of the "Star-Spangled Banner." I space out for a while, absorbed by the *New York Times Book Review*, until Lulu appears under the makeshift arbor, which is decorated with fake roses and garlands. Stiff, in a garish turquoise leotard trimmed with silver sequins and a matching hoop, she waits for her music to start, the adagio of a Brahms sonata, while her coach whispers last-minute advice. Behind the curtain, her teammates chant, "Go, Ludivine, Go!" Here she goes, hurtling herself across the floor, legs wide open, tossing the hoop which twirls in the air at a precarious angle, and lands, just short of foul, between her little outstretched hands. But she achieves a perfect fallback maneuver, one knee folded and the other leg stretched out, rolls into a ball and bounces up, hoop once more propelled upward, far away from her, and graciously floating down while she performs two speedy forward rolls which bring her in miraculous collision with the hoop in front of the jury at the exact moment the adagio reaches its conclusion. Bow. Exit on her tippy-toes, body rigid like a marionette. Wild applause, especially from me. "Bravo Ludivine! Bravo!"

From the corner of my eye I see Bill, on his way out of the auditorium. Navy blue sweater and T-shirt hanging loose over his jeans like a college boy. I sink out of sight behind the *Book Review*. Bill had seemed promising as a potential boyfriend when I had met him a few months earlier at another meet. Business journalist, recently split up from his wife. Andover. Harvard. His daughter a teammate of Lulu's. He had a nervous quirkiness that matched my own post-divorce seduction frenzy. When he pressed me against him on the sidewalk after our first date, my heart lifted in a moment of delicious hope. Unfortunately, his wife was from an "old, wealthy San Francisco family," and if she was going to take their daughters back to the West Coast, he would go back too. Still, I fantasized about him. I could glimpse the long shadows projected by our silhouettes in the sunset. After our third dinner date he gave me a long, passionate kiss in the cab, while his free hand fumbled under my skirt. Then I didn't hear from him again.

The whole day I try to avoid him, while shooting poisonous glances in his direction when he's not looking, until the prizes are handed out. By then he has disappeared. Perhaps his daughter hasn't won anything and they've hurried back to the city. Lulu, Corina, and I stay till the bitter end. First, second, and third place stand on a three-level podium, like winners at the Olympics. A little girl with huge blue eyes and hair the color of white gold, wins most of the competitions. A handsome man, with similar blue eyes and long dark hair gathered in a ponytail, rises to applaud her. They walk out together, the girl clutching a bunch of medals with blue and red ribbons, while he drapes his arms around her shoulders in a gesture that is both tender and a little awkward. My heart clenches at this display of fatherly tenderness, as if it's been hit by one of those poison arrows David brought back from the Amazon years ago and that are still hanging on a wall of my apartment.

"Who's that girl?"

"Oh, Dasha," Corina answers. "She's new."

"Where is she from?" I inquire, although it's obvious.

"Why do you want to know?" Lulu asks, alert to my slightest emotional shift.

"She's from Russia or the Ukraine I think," Corina says, before the two of them disappear, sucked out by the revolving door of the lobby. At the word Russia my cheeks turn hot, as if a corner of the veil hiding my secret tryst had been lifted.

# 6

April. The wide curves of the Merritt, so much lovelier than the deadly dull I-95. Manu Chao blaring on the sound system. The thrill of the open road, the intoxicating freedom. Pushing 80, surveying the grassy shoulders to spot the sheriffs' hidden cars. A shower suddenly spills out of the blue sky, lacing my windshield with a thousand silver drops. I slow down to read the exit numbers. When he gave me directions from the George Washington Bridge, Yuri was very precise, telling me almost to the minute how long it would take me to get to our meeting place, a rest area between exits 45 and 46, from where we'd head to a nearby motel. It's six PM, I've already been driving for two hours and twenty minutes and I must be getting close.

Exit 45. Here he is, standing near a gray Dodge van in the parking lot. From afar, in baggy jeans and a plaid flannel shirt hanging loose over his T-shirt, he looks just like another American guy. But up close, the stiffness of his posture and the intensity of his gaze contradict that first impression. No American holds himself that rigidly. He opens my car door and greets me with a plastic cup filled with blackcurrant juice. I laugh. Of course it's spiked with vodka. He watches me drink in silence. When I hand him the cup after a few sips, he puts his hand on my thigh and the same electric current hits me. "You look good," he says, his face expressionless. And then, without a pause: "Someone stole my tape-player. Or I lost it, I don't know. I'm pissed off. Wait, I want to show you something."

He brings me back a little green book from his van. On its edge the words *The Short Stories of Anton Chekhov* are engraved in tarnished silver type. A stamp on the title page reads WEST POINT LIBRARY.

West Point?

"You know Chekhov?" he asks me.

"I've seen some of his plays. *The Cherry Orchard, Uncle Vanya.*"

His eyes widen in surprise. "I learnt English with this book. I read original in Russian and English translation same time."

It's my turn to be surprised. I hadn't seen him in that light: a reader of Chekhov.

"Take it home. I want you to read it."

He gets back into his van and I follow him in the Saab for a few miles until we reach a Lucky 7 motel. He has me pull up to the side and around the back while he goes to the reception. In case the clerk might mistake me for a hooker? The idea gives me a cheap thrill. Maybe it's just motel etiquette. When he shows up in the room he throws me on the bed, lifts my tank top, pulls my breasts out of my bra, considers them with a somber look, and steps back. "Stay like this." His voice breathless. "Don't move." While he disappears outside, I wait for him, remaining the way he has arranged me, excited to be exposed, until he comes back and takes me to his van. We drive around for a few minutes, and he pulls up in the semi-deserted parking lot of a shopping mall. We climb over the seats and let ourselves drop at the back.

"I wanted to do it in the van," he says, pulling the curtains close.

Again, that tumbling into darkness, Yuri opening me up with his hands, his mouth, his sex until my boundaries dissolve, my limbs melt into his, into the van that contains us, in full view of the strip mall, yet secretly hidden by the closed curtains. The exciting fear that a cop might knock at the window winds us up to a pitch, like two teenagers sneaking out. Afterwards he gently cups my breasts. "The way I like them, fitting exactly into hands." As if he were appraising small melons. And his wicked smile, so close to my lips.

We are lying in the Dodge in the early evening. A reddish light filters around the windows. I kneel up, pull aside a curtain and look out. There's a small strip of stores, some already closed but all lit up with neon signs, a supermarket, a check-cashing place, a pizzeria, and an Arby's electric sign hanging from a tall post wishing GOOD MORNING and advertising a breakfast of blueberry pancakes and the name of a preacher coming on Sunday. An ordinary American strip-mall, the kind I find profoundly depressing, but that Yuri's presence magically imbues with exotic allure. The sense of dislocation and freedom is so intense that a surge of wild energy runs through me, making me almost faint.

"Let's sleep here," I whisper. "We could leave tomorrow morning and go for a ride. We could just go back to the motel later for my car. Don't you sleep in your van sometimes?"

46

He finds me funny, "you funny girl," but I can see from his face that he doesn't like the idea, that in his mind the van is not made to sleep in but to carry his merchandise. Besides, he has other plans. Dinner, for instance. He's starved.

In the morning, he turns on VH1 full blast and drags the sheet and blanket on the floor as he did our first time at Brighton Beach. He hates to have sex on beds, beds are boring. Ricky Martin's "La Vida Loca" is pumping into our ears with the same, frantic rhythm Yuri's going at me. *Her lips are devil red and her skin's the color mocha/she will wear you out livin' la vida loca, Come on!* Again, I feel something give inside of me under his multiple assaults. "You're letting yourself go, is good." He has a satisfied smile, as though he has been administering shock therapy and the results have exceeded his expectations.

Afterwards he goes to fill his thermos with coffee at the reception and comes back with a bag of muffins, also courtesy of the motel. We sit cross-legged and spread our breakfast on the sheet. He takes apart a cranberry muffin, and feeds it to me, bite after bite. The American coffee has never tasted so good. The light from the window falls on his forearm, caressing the pale blond hair on his wrist, and when he moves, his head turns into a golden halo. He circles my wrist with two fingers. "You're so tiny, like little girl," he says, almost tenderly.

When we're done with breakfast, and we've both gotten dressed, he opens the door, and gestures toward the trees lining the parking lot. "Look." He points to a branch blooming with flowers—I can't quite tell because I am so near-sighted. "My babies."

47

I put my glasses on to see better, and cannot believe my eyes: the "flowers" are the condoms we've used during the night.

"What? Are you out of your mind? Ewww!"

He roars with laughter at my discomfited face. "I didn't want to waste sperm. Sperm is good. Look, is dripping into soil."

"Please, get them out of there and throw them out!"

"OK, OK, I will."

I make a show of packing my bag in disgust, considering never seeing him again.

But when I pull out of my parking spot and watch him in my rear-view mirror, standing by his van, waving to me, I see the little blond boy with the curly hair from the photo, alone and sad, disconnected from his world. Behind him, the condoms are still hanging from the tree. From a distance they look poetic, like pale, translucent flowers, or jellyfish hung dry after a tidal wave.

***

I find *The Short Stories of Chekhov* at the bottom of my weekend bag, a few days later, while looking for a hairbrush. I had forgotten all about it. Tiny page markers torn off a notebook have been inserted between the pages of the story entitled "On the Way." I quickly jump to the first page flagged. In pencil, Yuri has underlined a passage spoken by a character named Likhartyoff.

"But I tell you that woman was and always will be the slave of man!" He said in a bass voice, thumping his fist upon the table. "She is wax—tender, plastic wax—from which man can mould what he will. . . . Devoted, unthinking slave! . . . The proudest, the most independent women—once I had succeeded in communicating to them my inspiration, came after me, unreasoning, asking no question, obeying my every wish."

What a declaration of intention! But also how clever—*romantic*, even—of Yuri to pass a message to me via Chekhov.

He calls me to ask if I have read the book, with the same eagerness as whether or not I'd drunk the wine from Moldavia. I don't need to lie this time, since I have read it—all of it. He quickly interrupts my literary commentary. All he wants to know is if I've read the part he has underlined. The part about women. What did I think of it?

I chuckle. "It's a little over the top, don't you think?"

"What it means?"

"Exaggerated, for effect. Provocative?"

He sounds ready to argue the night away, perhaps hoping there would be a meeting of our minds over this issue. After fifteen minutes, I am ready to hang up. He can fantasize all he wants about molding a woman to his will, but he's got the wrong woman.

"Goodnight Yuri. How do you say that again in Russian?"

"*Spokoinyi nochi*," he answers reluctantly.

"*Spokoinyi nochi*," I repeat, and I hang up.

# 7

The meeting with my editor has been rescheduled twice, once by me, trying to buy extra time, the second time by him, because he was taking a week off in the Fiji Islands. So when the phone rings, the morning of the day we are to meet for lunch, I half expect his assistant to cancel, but it's Yuri, inviting me back to Brighton Beach. The sight of the condoms fluttering in the wind, no matter how poetic, has seriously cooled me off, but he sounds so unflappable, so sure of himself, that his opening question, "Are you still alive?" cracks me up. The phone rings immediately after I hang up, and it's my editor this time, to confirm our lunch at a restaurant near Lincoln Center. I try to pass off my giddy "Hi" as excitement to talk about my manuscript, which is far from the truth, since I have made very little progress. This is particularly worrisome, since my advance on royalties is linked to my delivering chapters at regular intervals.

Sitting on a banquette, in his pale blue shirt and well-cut tweed jacket, his face framed by retro, black, rectangular glasses, my editor looks so impeccably preppy that I feel duplicitous, not only because I can't show him even a few chapters of my manuscript, but because instead of writing

I have been wasting my weekends with a *louche* character from Moscow who, for sport, festoons trees with used condoms, although I kind of get a kick from the contrast between the two. I stay vague on the subject of Mimi, the *café-concert* singer who has lately been sneaking out of the Governor's mansion to meet with her Vietnamese lover in a back alley of the Chinese town, and divert his attention to exotic details, like the rituals of opium smoking. I knead a piece of bread dough into a tiny ball and balance it at the tip of my index finger.

"Like this, in a long bamboo pipe."

My editor leans back in his chair and pushes his cup of coffee aside.

"You slip a little wood pillow under your head, you lie down and pfffft! You're off."

Through the open collar of his perfect chambray shirt (Paul Smith? Agnès B.?) I notice a beauty mark near his right collarbone.

"Wood pillow, huh? A little hard isn't it?"

Did I just detect a British accent, or is it Australian? Did I miss something? My interest perks up. I fantasize about dating him for a second.

"Right. There's a scene in which Mimi is initiated to opium smoking by her lover, Nguyen Linh. It's just before dawn and you can hear the sounds of roosters in the market."

"So when can I read some of those scenes?"

I stir my coffee, which doesn't need any stirring because I don't take sugar, and stall. "You know *Confessions of an English Opium-Eater*, right?"

"Thomas De Quincey? Yes."

"I have found French accounts that are even more intriguing, and hundred-year-old photos. I keep incorporating new details. It slows me down."

The beauty mark has reappeared inside the open collar of his shirt. The waiter discreetly places the tray with the check near his elbow and just as discreetly, my editor slips his Amex card underneath, then looks at me, pensive. I fashion another ball of bread dough the size of an opium pellet and imagine kissing him in the hollow underneath the Adam's apple.

"You should go there."

"Where? To Vietnam?

"I think that's what you need. At a certain point you've got to forget your research and *let yourself go*. I don't think you'll be able to write until you go there. I'll give you my guidebooks," he adds while scribbling his signature on the credit card slip. "I was there last winter with my wife."

So much for my seduction attempt. Let yourself go. Weren't these the very words that Yuri had used—albeit in a very different context? I repress a smile.

"What?"

"Nothing."

Instead of jumping into a cab, he suggests walking back through the park, which surprises me—doesn't he have urgent decisions to make on a book jacket, blurbs to collect for a back cover, galleys to prepare? Is he playing hooky? He laughs at my suggestion.

The weather seems to have miraculously turned to spring during our lunch, the park having exploded into a gossamer cloud of pink and white blossoms against a sky of tender blue.

"Isn't the park wonderful at this time of year?"

I am one of these fiercely downtown people who, living in the East Village, rarely set foot above Fourteenth Street, as though uptown were another dreary planet, way too dull to visit. Actually one of the last times I went to the park was one gloomy November afternoon with David a few weeks before the end. We sat down among the dead leaves on a little hill overlooking the lake and I blurted out for no reason, "I don't see myself growing old in the States." David stood up. His silhouette filled the sky, already fading. Hands in pockets, shoulders thrown back, his posture was almost defiant. I can only imagine now what he was thinking: *Well, you're not going to grow old with me anyway, so what do I care?* The memory of that moment still stings.

"Vietnam," my editor repeats, as we say goodbye by the statue of General Sherman. "That's the key."

# 8

May. I am meeting Yuri in front of Café Moscow in Brighton Beach. He's pacing up and down the boardwalk in his big black leather coat, a blond giant with pale eyes who grabs me by the wrist and flattens a violent kiss on my closed lips. Spring hasn't yet reached South Brooklyn, which is still on Russian weather. The gusts of wind are icy. After a quick dinner at the restaurant, half-empty except for four mustachioed men furiously smoking and arguing at a table behind a window, Yuri marches us to a newsstand at the corner of Brighton Beach Avenue and Ocean Parkway to "look at American magazines." He steps over the stacks of *Argumenti i Fakti*, *Novi Russki Slovo*, *Russki Bazar*, and *Russkaya Reklama* which cram the front of the shop, and brandishes a copy of *Marie Claire* with Demi Moore on the cover.

"Look at her eyes," he says, staring into them for a moment before putting the magazine back. "And here's my ideal woman." He picks up Vogue and sticks it in front of me. "Catherine Zeta-Jones. Look. Long black hair, hazel eyes, that's my type. *Goooorgeous!*" The elongated Russian "o" comes off with a hint of sarcasm.

Although my curly, reddish hair clearly puts me in a

different type, I take no offense. Let him dream on! I just find it slightly annoying that he can't keep his fantasies to himself. At least, they reassure me that I am only in passing in his life, that sooner or later a woman with long black hair will sweep him off his feet. I am so out of place, so obviously a Western tourist wandering in his world out of curiosity, that I almost wish one of those *goooorgeous* creatures would spirit him away and release me from his grip.

Back in his room, he enters me without warning, while I stand at the window, peering into the dark ocean. I still have my coat and boots on. He pops open the buttons of my coat and pulls up my sweater and my bra, then pulls down my pants and hits the small of my back with a sharp little tap to make me bend lower and assure the best angle for penetration.

In the windowpane I see the reflection of my breasts dipping into his hands like pale moons, and a giant shadow toiling over me. We drop to the ground, both in our coats and shoes, with only that strip of flesh between our waists and knees exposed, more ravishingly naked for being surrounded by layers of clothes, and we start again, him going at me in long, hammering moves until I cry out and he shoves his hand against my mouth to smother my scream and collapses on my stomach, his weight crushing me.

Russian music plays in a loop. A woman singer this time. Deep, wrenching voice. He pours vodka into two glasses and drinks a shot. I don't touch mine. His left arm curls around me. With his right hand he lights up a Parliament and softly blows out the smoke.

"I am illegal, I told you that?"

"Yes."

Another pull on his cigarette.

"I told you about Russian woman right? The one I am going to marry?" He glances at me sideways. "I move in with her. We went to pick furniture together. We found apartment in New Jersey." He turns toward me. "For INS, you understand. Is not about sex. Maybe she wants me, sometimes I think, the way she looks at me, I don't know. But I don't want her."

"I know I know. I got my papers that way too."

"You got married for papers?"

"David and I got married for the green card" is what I used to say when people asked us, with that flippant tone that set David on edge, even though he, too, sometimes said, ironically, "We got married 'for the green card,'" quote-unquote, mimicking me. We had done it furtively, at City Hall, with two friends as witnesses, without telling either of our families. I had insisted on keeping it quiet, especially secret from my mother. David had been married before. He had his own misgivings. As for me, since my mother had never married, I had decided, proudly, that I wasn't going to play the farce of a "bourgeois marriage," by the same token denying my mother the redemption that she might have longed for. Funny how wickedly our unconscious can play both sides and the middle simultaneously. On my birth certificate, on the line saying "father," instead of a name, the word inconnu was written: unknown. I could never be legitimate anyway. It was too late for that. Marriage for me had too much baggage. I wanted to keep our relationship pure, just about love. "Romantic." I was a romantic by default.

"That's how I got my green card. But we were in love."

He sniggers and pours himself another shot of vodka and downs it, head tilted back.

"I have only loved one woman in my life. My mother."

I move a little from him to disengage myself from his arm. "I know. You told me. You don't know what love is yet."

He puts out his cigarette and wraps his arms around me again. "I got into sex before I had a chance to fall in love."

# 9

The rhythmic gymnastics season is over. Weekends, Lulu goes to her dad's, and I meet up with Yuri. He talks about taking me to Cape Cod when the weather turns warm. I think school will be over in a month and I will soon be in France with Lulu to visit my mother, and that Yuri and I will never make it past the summer. But I don't say anything. These are not real plans anyway, just dreams, puffs of smoke. Mostly we meet at motels in Maryland or in New Jersey near where Yuri attends his arts and crafts fairs, like a couple of fugitives on the lam. The motels are more exciting to me than a trip to Cape Cod anyway. They all look the same, although they belong to different chains: Lucky 7. Super 8. International Motel. EconoLodge. They are located in strip-malls, right off the highway, sometimes tucked away within a cluster of other motels and restaurants. Yuri checks in at the reception, while I park my car at the bedroom door and slip in incognito. I love Yuri's willingness to be involved with me without making any demands, just as I love the motels for their anonymity. To me they are the true symbols of American freedom. I want them to be as plain and nondescript, as characterless as possible. I want a certain feeling of seediness. A certain shade of neglect. I disappear from myself more that way. I don't tell Yuri about those fantasies. He would find them perverse, attributing them to my decadent western upbringing. He, on the other hand, holds these rooms to certain standards. He likes some better than others. He finds some cleaner, others dirtier, although to my eyes they seem interchangeable. He frets about the dust, runs a finger on the dresser like a fussy housewife, picks up my bra and my underwear off the floor, checks the towels in the bathroom, makes sure the glasses have been properly wrapped in paper. Meanwhile, I lay on the bed, studying the intricate pattern of the bedspread, analyzing the various shades of green in the wallpaper, marveling at the muddiness of the colors, at their aggressive dullness, waiting for him to finish his inspection and spread my legs open.

I watch him come out of the shower, a small towel loosely knotted around his hips, his shoulders pink from the hot water. We are in a motel upstate somewhere, not a real place, just an exit number off the thruway. He crosses the room and sits at the table, where he contemplates a pile of bills, his left hand toiling with a calculator, then launches into a long tirade about a Russian woman he has run into the previous weekend at another fair, a "goooorgeous" woman, whom he had fucked a couple of years earlier, and who had just dropped by "out of the blue" at his stand. Then he counts the money he's made for the day. The fair goes on tomorrow and he is calculating how much he needs to make to pay off his credit card debt. My mind wandering, I contemplate the green arabesques of the wallpaper, which clash with the dull blue plaid pattern of the bedspread.

"Show me how you touch yourself." He abruptly turns to me, his hands still on the calculator. "Spread your legs."

Like a stern examiner judging a performance, he watches as I wet a finger on my tongue, then insert it inside of me.

"Show me how you do it."

The brusqueness of his orders arouses me. The vulnerability of my lower body, naked, my shirt barely grazing my navel, while he sits businesslike in front of his bills, is exciting.

"Don't stop." He watches me to make sure I don't slack off on the job. Then he comes closer and sits on the bed, opening me up with two fingers and peering between my legs.

"I want to see your hole."

I come on his hand.

He is back at his desk, ever the businessman, albeit naked and smoking a Parliament, adding up numbers on a piece of paper, calculator at his elbow. I pack my toilet bag in the bathroom, check that I have my cell phone and keys, lace up my espadrilles, sling my weekend bag over my shoulder. He lifts his head from his papers and watches me get ready.

"Don't get addicted to me," he warns me.

Addicted? I don't even think about him when I am back home, until it's time to see him again. Puzzled, I look at him for a moment, then go up to him, pull the cigarette out of his mouth, take a puff off of it and stick it back between his lips.

"How about you?"

He stares at me, his eyebrows knitted, pinches the cigarette between his thumb and forefinger and tosses it into the wastebasket.

"Don't worry about me."

I don't hear from Yuri for a whole week after that. I leave a couple of messages on his cell phone, which he doesn't return, not his usual M.O. In his own way, Yuri is reliable, if not punctual. Something must be amiss. No news over the weekend either. When he finally calls the following Monday, he announces himself formally as "Yuri." Not "Yuri the Russian guy." Nor "Yura," his nickname. It's not his usual late-night time either, but right after dinner before I have a chance to put Lulu to bed.

"Is something wrong?"

"I have to stop seeing you." His voice is loaded with tragic undertones, a hero regretfully submitting to his fate.

I try to keep my *sangfroid*. "Why?"

A tiny explosion of joy dissipates his mournful tone. "I am getting married."

"I know. You told me."

"No. I'm getting married *for love*."

Getting married for love? Another one of his nauseating clichés. Who is she? It can't be the same woman he was supposed to marry "for his papers," is it? The one he was going to move in with and with whom he had bought furniture? That one, I know, was strictly "business." No, he explains, this one is a former dancer, a "beauty" with long black hair, "*gooorgeous.*"

"The woman who was at the fair the weekend before I saw you?" I stick a strand of hair in my mouth and chew

61

on it as a way to ease the tightening in my chest.

"Yes." I nibble the little strand of hair till it turns as hard as a little blade.

"You mean you'd slept with her then? Before we met at the motel a week prior?"

"Correct." He tries to sound contrite, but he can't help gushing. "Tasha" is US citizen. "Tasha" has money from ex-husband. "Tasha" drives second-hand Jaguar.

"So you're giving up on the ultra-long Mercedes?"

He ignores my barb. They're looking at houses and schools upstate to move in with daughter. (Oh, she has a daughter too?) They're going to have a kid. A son. His voice is jubilant.

I have been with Yuri for the adventure, not for the long haul. I had already envisioned the black-haired girl who would sweep him off his feet and release me. Here she is, just sooner than I thought. I pick up the little amber frog he's given me, which is crouching on the base of my desk lamp, a token of affection from our first night together, and press it hard into my palm.

"You're hurting me." I can't find anything else to say, ashamed to even reveal that much vulnerability to him.

"I know." He tries to console me: we could still see each other when he comes to the city. But we couldn't have sex. He wants to be a good, loyal husband.

Another cloying cliché! Spare me! "At least, make sure you get your green card out of this."

*That* makes him squirm and he protests, putting on his most sanctimonious tone.

"I am marrying *for love*, not for papers."

"Oh right, right! OK that's enough. Bye."

I hang up. At least Yuri has given me what I wanted: one last reckless affair, before settling down again with some as yet impossible-to-imagine "right man." Maybe it's for the best. To end before we got attached to each other. The phone rings again but I let the answering machine pick up. He doesn't leave a message. I pitch the amber frog at the bottom of my desk drawer hoping it will break, but, like some vulgar piece of plastic, it doesn't.

II

## 1

The day before the 4th of July, Lulu and I fly to Nice to spend the summer, as we usually do, in the small Provence village perched among the vineyards of the Estérel Mountains, where my mother lives half the year. It's a lovely village, but far from the seashore, which is hard to reach in the summertime with all the traffic jams along the coast, and after a while the days start to drag on and Lulu gets bored. I dutifully report back to my laptop every morning to work on my novel and stay put until lunch, although I find myself unable to chase away the image of Yuri floating behind the backdrop of Saigon, like some gigantic shadow puppet. Alarmingly, he even starts to invade Nguyen Linh, Mimi's whippet-thin and indolent Vietnamese lover, with his personality tics and massive physical presence.

On Sundays, we take my rental car and drive to a hotel—an old American barracks from WWII, long fallen into disrepair and recently converted into a luxury compound—which has a very nice pool, as well as a pond inhabited by a family of small ducks. Even though the pool is normally reserved for the hotel clientele, the staff makes an exception for my mother, the eccentric lady with the big, floppy straw hat who does laps and reads in the

67

shade, smoking her Benson & Hedges. My mother and I each order a *panaché*—a beer mixed with lemon soda— while Lulu gets a coke in the original glass bottle, and we lie down on deckchairs under a parasol.

One Sunday afternoon as we are lounging in the shade of the verandah after a lunch of grilled fish, feeling in a particularly expansive mood, I tell my mother about Yuri. I've always told her about the men I've been involved with, at least the most important ones or those whom I figure will arouse her interest. In the crackling summer heat the pine trees give off a strong smell of resin. The deep blue of the sky shines so brightly it hurts the eyes.

"Anyway, it wasn't meant to become a relationship. It's probably just as well that it ended like this."

She looks at me, waiting to hear more. Her green eyes, her exquisite, straight nose and wide cheekbones are handsomely framed by the brim of her straw hat

"He is a hothead," I tell her. "But it takes guts to do what he's doing, surviving in the States with no money and no papers, trying to have a go at it." I glance toward Lulu, who's busy feeding the ducks with bits of leftover baguette from our lunch, and steal a cigarette from my mother's pack.

"He must be interesting then." She leans forward to light a cigarette of her own and blows the smoke through her nostrils. She is a hothead herself, my mother, and she's got plenty of guts. In fact, there are more than a few common points between Yuri and her: their street language, their ruggedness, their penchant for provocation. A Russophile, she used to take me to the Russian ballets when they came to the Paris Opera, and her bookcases are filled with novels by Vassili Grossman, Alexandr Soljenitsin, and Andrei Makine. Not to mention her earlier flirtation with the French Communist Party in the fifties. We sit for a moment, lying in parallel deckchairs, each holding a cigarette in our right hand in the oppressive Mediterranean heat, deafened by the buzz of the cicadas. These are our best moments together, when we are not ripping each other apart over the past, over her shortcomings as a mother, over my shortcomings as a daughter, over the fact that I never had a father: when we talk about men. Some of the only times when I feel we are truly bonding.

Lulu's head suddenly appears from behind the fence of boxwood separating the pond from the swimming-pool area and I quickly stub my cigarette.

My mother laughs with disdain, and makes a show of blowing rings of smoke. She's an expert at smoke rings. They curl into one another in a graceful blue spiral that becomes smaller and smaller until it vanishes into the air.

"Don't let her dictate what you can do or can't do. She's already turning into an American kid who pulls her mother by the nose. What's wrong with smoking a cigarette once in a while?"

I stiffen at my mother's tone. Lulu has always "pulled me by the nose." And yes, she is an American kid. Three other children are jumping in and out of the water under the indolent eyes of their parents, who are sunbathing on the opposite, sunny side of the pool, and she dives in. The water splashes all over our feet. I turn the conversation back to Yuri. I may be weak, but at least I can show my mother that I haven't become one of those dreaded *bourgeoises* we both abhor, that I, too, now that I am single and free, can hold my own in front of her. Talking about Yuri with my mother gives him a weird kind of legitimacy and a certain aura, as if he were an outlaw hero. Especially now that he is at a safe distance, a character in a world that couldn't be more alien to Provence.

## 2

October. The French summer has come and gone, taking away the memory of long afternoons at the pool, the round of martins in the sunset sky, and the sweet scent of fig trees. I am waiting for Lulu at her school. The lobby is deserted, except for the few parents waiting to pick up the girls from rhythmic gymnastics practice. I sit on the long bench with them, exchanging a few polite and meaningless comments to pass the time. We have just switched to wintertime and night takes us by surprise. My cell phone rings. Startled, I see Yuri's name appear on the screen. I had not removed his number from the phone. I get up and walk to the other end of the lobby. He is in New York. Can he stop by and see me? It's over.

My heart jumps. "What's over?"

"Marriage over."

I stay speechless, although not entirely surprised, while a sick excitement rises in my stomach.

"I'm in city. Can I see you?"

"Now? I'm picking my daughter up at school."

I've never let Yuri come to my place. It's been off-limits from the beginning. And now hardly seems the right time, just as he reappears after a four months' marriage. But in spite of myself, my mind immediately starts making plans. Since I drive Lulu to David's after practice on Friday nights and pick her up on Sunday evenings, I will be alone all weekend.

Like a little rocket equipped with a homing device, Lulu erupts from the staircase with a group of girls, hurtling into the lobby in a great commotion of hoops, scarves flying, and sports bags noisily dropped, and collapses on my lap, out of breath. She's starved, can she go get a candy bar at the vending machines? "Please, please, please, little *maman chérie* with a cherry on top?" She playfully presses her index finger on my nose to make me smile. I shake my head no, and hold her tight in my arms, kiss her on her forehead and ruffle her hair to soften my refusal. It's too late, almost dinnertime, and I have to drive her to her dad's.

"I want to see you," Yuri is saying on the phone, in that sexually charged voice that used to get my heart racing.

"Please, please, *Maman*," Lulu insists. "*S'il-te-plaît.*"

"OK, go. A small one, OK?"

"Wait," I say to Yuri, and hand Lulu a dollar bill.

"Who are you talking to?" she asks before bolting to the vending machines, abandoning her backpack and hoop at my feet, not waiting for an answer.

"What happened?" I ask into the phone.

"I explain later. Can I come tonight?"

That's all it takes.

On the FDR drive, along the East River, a yellow and grotesquely large full moon looking like a cardboard cutout for a children's show is rising on the Brooklyn bank above the Domino sugar sign. In the rearview mirror Ludivine is slumbering on the back seat, her head hanging sideways over her scarf. The little bit of dribble at the corner of her open mouth fills me with tenderness. She's asleep by the time I pull up in front of David's apartment building in the Village and he comes down to carry her up.

* * *

Yuri is gaunt, which makes him look great, all dressed in black—in jeans and a sweater he bought at a T.J. Maxx bargain mall in New Jersey where he'd dragged me one afternoon in the spring—as if he were going to a funeral. Suffering (or weight loss) gives him a kind of tragic dignity that he didn't have before, when he was all vulgar joviality and crude energy. I put on a CD of the band Cowboy Junkies to complement the dark and somber mood. Not quite Vusotsky, but he likes it. He's sitting there on my white couch, his long legs folded to the side, looking around my apartment, commenting on how big it is.

"I bought it with my ex-husband for nothing," I tell him, "Nobody wanted to live this far east. It was too dangerous."

"Maybe it would look good if you had modern furniture," he says dryly, taking in the 1930s piano and the art deco coffee table.

I, for my part, am surprised that the end of such a short marriage would have shaken him up that much, but I am moved all the same. Whether it was his ego or true love, his pushy and oversexed persona is toned down a notch. I take pity on him and bring him the chilled bottle of vodka I always keep in the freezer.

"Oh, you're a drinker."

I laugh. "No! But I keep it for whenever I have a party or friends over for dinner."

He looks doubtful, as if he can't imagine what kind of person would keep liquor in the house for some future festivity, instead of drinking it all up as soon as it's bought.

He lies down with me in my bed with his black socks and black briefs. "No sex," he announces in a mournful tone, flicking his limp penis. "I'm finished." In the middle of the night I wake up to the sound of Russian hurriedly spoken on the phone in my study. He comes back muttering something about having to "call Moscow" to catch his "business partners" while it's morning over there and not to worry, he's used phone card. When I wake up again it's morning in New York and Yuri is lying next to me, asleep on his back. I lean on one elbow to look at him. Again, from above, the stubborn forehead and the small but strong chin, the long, thin mouth that looks both sensual and cruel. Again the idea that he shouldn't be here, that he doesn't belong, that he should leave as soon as he wakes up. But he opens his eyes with a sly smile—he might have pretended to be asleep to catch me off guard— and grabs me between the legs.

"No!" I scream, not convincingly.

He has me in a vice-grip, his hand in my panties, his thumb already rummaging inside of me, getting me wet as though he had access to some part of my brain that commands my sexuality and has the power to turn it on and off as he pleases.

He gives me the details of the breakup later when

I bring two cups of coffee to my bedroom. It involved a bout of angry mood for his part, at the door of a crafts fair in which he was a vendor, and which resulted in his being thrown out—all because Tasha had provoked him and made him jealous. Whereupon she had immediately filed for divorce. Although his convoluted explanations suggest a violent temper—clearly Tasha had decided she wanted no life with this loose cannon—I choose to believe his version: Tasha had overreacted. Tasha is bitch. I don't mind his ranting and venting. He isn't as cocky as he used to be. The collapse of his dream is humbling him. And he has, after all, come back to me. Even if I am only his default position, I can't help but feel the pinch of victory. There were other reasons for the breakup, he explains: they had talked about starting a family together, and then Tasha had backed off and decided she didn't want any more children. Her daughter was fourteen, they would have grandchildren instead. Yuri was furious—"She had promised!"—he had always been dreaming of a son. Girls always grew up to be "bitches." But OK, he went along with it. Then Tasha made him jealous, calling him from bars or restaurants, surrounded by men, and—he was convinced—flirting with them.

He pulls a manila folder out of the leather briefcase he's brought with him. Various official looking documents and an envelope bulging with photos spill out of it.

"I want you to tell me what you think of her."

Part of me doesn't want to look at the evidence of his "love marriage," part of me—the voyeur part—is dying to look at them. I hold out my hand.

She is sexy—undeniably—in a kind of slutty way:

75

impossibly long legs, dancer's posture, voluptuous black mane cascading down her back, wide cheekbones, pale eyes drowned in smoky eye shadow, and a mouth that manages to be both sensual and hard. Here she is, the black-haired creature who has swept him off his feet, leaning against the prow of a Jaguar, in high-heeled, strappy sandals and mini-mini skirt, her face thrown to the side, offering a side-long look at the photographer (him?), her arms raised in a circle above her head as if she were auditioning for a job as a go-go dancer.

"She is beautiful, isn't she?" His voice trails off as he loses himself in reverie over her image.

"Well, frankly. . . ." I place the photo back on top of the others. "She is a little too—," I hesitate, not wanting to sound too critical or jealous—"too done up for my taste."

"She has classical ballet training," he adds dreamily. "I couldn't get enough of her. . . ."

I put my hand up, but there's no stopping him.

"Eight, nine orgasms a night. . . . She couldn't get enough of me either. And she wasn't faking, believe me."

I briefly try to remember how many orgasms a night I've had with him, then pick up the other photos. Here they are, in front of a priest. She is still perched in her stilettos, which bring her close to his height, in a sexy, shimmering white suit, carrying a bouquet of lilies, her hair in an elaborate updo, and him with a black turtleneck and a suit, his hair gelled back. On the next picture they kiss, *yeux dans les yeux*. She's probably only a few years older than he is, but her face is already so hardened that he looks innocent at her side, his own features plain and open. Again, his expression reminds me of the little boy in his mother's arms in the picture he had showed me months earlier. Now she's posing in a strapless top and the tight skirt, minus the jacket, standing on the stoop of a white, clapboard house, in three-quarter profile, one foot pointing forward and shoulders thrown back, in a classic pinup pose.

A few other pictures have been taken in the garden of a hotel and on a cliff overlooking the ocean—perhaps during their honeymoon. Cape Cod? Tasha wearing a pair of shorts and high-heeled sandals showing her long legs to advantage, a striped sailor boat-neck shirt and a pair of oversized sunglasses. Tasha sitting on the hood of the Jaguar. Again, the pinup pose, knees folded high and hands resting behind her back, pushing her chest forward, with the poised expression of a woman who knows how to get what she wants from men. I slip the pictures back in the folder with a twinge of jealousy, at the same time appalled to find myself Tasha's successor—or predecessor—or both, actually.

Yuri has lit up a cigarette and watches me.

"So? What you say?"

There's too much to say.

"Maybe it's just as well that the marriage is over."

"Why you say that?" He is hanging on to my every word.

"Because she looks so . . . tough." I feel sorry for him. For all his provocative stance and sexual self-confidence, he doesn't know how to play the cards life has handed him, which could have given him what he needs so badly: love and legitimacy. He stubs his cigarette in the saucer of his coffee cup.

"She's fucking bitch."

Among the papers are his marriage certificate and a letter she has sent him threatening to denounce him to the INS if he doesn't accept the divorce. It's blackmail, but maybe that is the only way to deal with a Yuri. Or maybe it's the Russian way.

"But why? Did you refuse to divorce her?"

His eyes turn cloudy.

"I wanted to stay married long enough to get papers."

"I thought it was true love?" I ask, sarcastic.

He picks up the pillow and punches it so hard a little puff of duvet escapes from the pillowcase and alights on his cheek. He brushes it aside angrily.

"Don't. Don't start."

I glance at the marriage certificate. Natalia Nikolaievna M. By a strange coincidence, she was born the same day in September as me. I ask him if we have anything in common.

He looks at me and shakes his head.

"No. Nothing."

"I mean, personality-wise?"

"You're not bitch," he says after a long, ruminative silence.

I don't take it as a compliment, but rather that I have been too soft on him.

When I come out of the shower, Yuri isn't in my bedroom anymore. He has rolled out a yoga mat in the middle of the living room and is propelled on one fist, resting on the strength of just one arm, muscles taut and sinewy, his whole body levitating above it, parallel to the floor, flat as a plank of wood—an amazing feat, considering he weighs about 185 lbs. from his own admission. I watch him in silence. After two or three minutes he lowers himself down on the mat, slowly and with perfect control of his movements.

"Wow! That was something! I didn't know you did yoga."

He grins with pride, seeing from my look of astonishment that his show has been a total success. Then he slowly raises himself on his shoulders and head, and balances on the tip of his head, body perpendicular to the ground perfectly straight, his shirt falling over his head, revealing his taut stomach.

Stunning! But the appearance of the yoga mat and of his big body levitating in the middle of my living room—along with the teapot I discover sitting on the kitchen table under a dishcloth to keep it warm, sends me a chill: Yuri is making himself at home. What if Lulu walked in and saw this big, blond, brutal-looking man standing on his head, his pair of size 13 Adidas sandals lying by the mat?

## 3

Yuri's just moved to New Jersey, halfway between Philadelphia and Atlantic City. I like that distance between us, knowing that he is safely tucked away, two hours from Manhattan, an ocean of land between us which I can cross, stereo cranked up, my mind a blur. I bang the car door and turn on the key. Press on the gas, ease off the clutch, first gear clicks into place, takeoff smooth as a dream. Houston Street. Holland Tunnel. The Turnpike. The Garden State. The old, trusty Saab negotiates the curves of the parkway in a supple, steady rhythm as if the white line marking each lane were a railway track to which it was hitched. I get off the parkway, follow his directions, and glimpse his tall silhouette standing by the side of the road, waving at me so that I don't miss his driveway, which is tucked behind a boulder.

Like the proud owner of a country house, he gives me a tour of the property. By the garage, his gray Dodge van sits by a white Lincoln sedan—also his. Beyond the driveway, all over the large backyard, carcasses of old cars litter the wild grass. They belong to his landlord. Sparrows dart about a wooden picnic table and a pair of folding metal chairs. One alights on the table, pecks the wood a couple of times, looks disoriented for a moment and takes off. The big, clapboard Victorian house is painted a garish hot pink. His apartment is on the ground floor.

He opens the door with a flourish. A narrow hallway cluttered with boxes. A living room dominated by a desk and a massive Naugahyde swivel-chair fit for a CEO, clashing with a baroque, fake Louis XV sofa upholstered in gold and ivory brocade, and a pair of matching, dainty gilded armchairs, which I assume are left over from the set he bought when he was planning to keep house with his first Russian fiancée. On a bookcase filled with nesting dolls and a menagerie of tiny glass-blown and amber animals like the frog he had offered me in Brooklyn, a copy of Dale Carnegie's *How to Win Friends and Influence People* and a handful of Russian classics—*The Brothers Karamazov*, *War and Peace*, *Anna Karenina*, *Dead Souls*. He points to the view of trees and grass from the living room windows. "My little country house." Actually, the whole place has a certain seedy charm, if you are the kind of person who finds charm in seediness, with the rusted electric coils on the stove, the cracked linoleum, the boom box on the counter, the bare bulbs hanging from the ceiling, his sleeping bag in lieu of a bedspread—not unlike the motels where we used to meet.

I unpack the cheese, the loaf of French bread and the bottle of *Pomerol* I've brought with me. Yuri puts everything away—"for dinner, later" —takes a quart of vodka and a tin of black caviar out of the freezer and proceeds to saw the caviar with a serrated knife as if it were a slab of frozen ground beef.

"Keeps longer this way," he mutters, feeding it to

81

me with the tip of the knife before tossing me on the Louis XV couch with casual possessiveness.

Later we lay down on the bed under the sleeping bag. The afternoon's pale sun has long ago crept out. Through the half-open window, smells of wood burning and of wet soil waft in, not the countryside of elegantly renovated farmhouses, but the no man's land of drifters, a mysterious world I know nothing about. Again, the excitement of being on the lam from my life. The silence of the night envelops us, an inky darkness darker than the night in Manhattan.

I wake up early the next morning and make my way between Yuri's "merchandise" stacked in cardboard boxes in the hallway to look out the front door. It has rained during the night and puddles stretch lazily around. On the periphery of the yard the broken cars emerge from the wet grass like skeletons of prehistoric animals shaking off the morning dew. In front of the garage, Yuri's gray Dodge and his white Lincoln are parked cheek to jowl with my Saab, also glistening with raindrops, the windshield and windows misted. If I left my car there, would it turn, in time, into a prehistoric animal too?

I tiptoe back in and slip under the sleeping bag along Yuri's warm body. He groans and throws his arm around me. His massive shoulders are covered with light freckles. The hair above his thick neck is buzzed high in a military cut. I gently run my fingers at the edge of the stubble.

When we get up later I notice a framed picture of Yuri as a little boy in his mother's arms on the dresser, the same picture he had shown me in Brighton Beach. I pick it up. He looks like a boy to whom a mom would say, "My little angel," "Sweetie," or any of the equivalent Russian terms of endearment.

"What are you doing?" Yuri asks, with a menacing tone.

I put the picture back. "Nothing."

"I was four or five. We still in Tbilisi, living with grandparents."

"I was raised by my mother and grandparents too," I say, intrigued by the coincidence.

He swats the air with his hand: so what. He slept in grandmother's room, on a foldable cot, he says. Sometimes he heard sounds from mother's room. Once he heard banging, furniture being dragged, screams. When he went into the room later he thought he saw dark, brown spots on the wall, like dried blood, but he always made things up. He had too much imagination. Maybe the spots had always been there. He read all the time, a lonely, shy boy, until his mother sent him to swimming lessons, afraid he would turn into a girly boy.

"Ha ha! No need to worry about that."

"No, is true. I was really shy and lonely. At home all the time. Swimming saved my life."

He was a natural. He had a swimmer's body, long legs and wide shoulders. In no time he was winning competitions, local, then regional. He joined the Georgian national team. He was headed for the Olympics when the country collapsed. I imagine him waking up at dawn on Saturday mornings to go to practice, like Lulu. He loved the team camaraderie. The coach was tough, he punished them if they didn't push themselves beyond their limits, but Yuri craved male authority. "Tough love, that's what boy needs." It was the best time in his life. And then his mother died.

He leans over to light a cigarette and stays silent for a while, collecting the ashes in the palm of his hand. It's as if there were two Yuris: a sweet, bookish, sensitive, imaginative boy, and a carnal, brutal man, and the two of them couldn't fit properly together.

"How did she die?"

He smokes without answering. Finally, he says: "Accident." He was in the dacha with his grandmother when it happened. It was wintertime. He had just turned eleven. Since then he goes every year on the anniversary of her death to put flowers on her grave. Her favorite flowers, lilies. But now he can't. He's stuck here. He twists his shoulders and punches the wood frame of the bed behind him, spilling a little of the ashes on his pillow.

"Like fucking jail here."

"Is that why you want to go to Moscow so bad?"

"I miss it. I don't want to live there. I just want to go and come back. Is all I want." He remains silent for a moment. "For Jews, no problem immigrating."

"What do you mean?"

"Most of Russians here, they all Jews. They come here, they say they were persecuted in the ex-Soviet Union and they become legal right away. They have associations of Jews that help them. I went to see them. They told me to just pretend to be Jew." He snorts with disgust. "I'd never do that. I'd rather die."

A cold sweat runs down my back. Thinking of David and of Lulu, who, by virtue of being David's daughter, is half-Jewish. The brutal Yuri has come back. With his pale hair, his buzz cut, his gray eyes, he would make the perfect Nazi.

Evening. We are still in the same play. Russian, kitchen-sink, realistic drama. Leftovers of cheese and caviar and the teapot on one side of the kitchen table. Display trays stacked on the other side. He hands me a soft cloth with a sardonic grin. "Woman's job. Can you clean for me?" He runs his finger on the brooches to show the dust. They are hand-painted with miniature scenes in the same style as the traditional Russian jewelry boxes made of lacquered wood. "I want them clean for fair next weekend." He removes one brooch, carefully wipes it and pins it back. "Like that. Think you can do it?"

"No. I'm tired. I'll give you a hand tomorrow." I put the cloth aside. He pushes it back into my hand.

Chekhov's quote flashes in my mind. "She is wax— tender, plastic wax—from which man can mould what he will. . . ." I long for my Saab, parked in the driveway. I should have left after his remarks about the Jews. And now it must be eleven or midnight and I don't have the energy to leave. With my bad eyesight, I hate to drive in the dark. The night seems even inkier than the night before, as if we were sinking deeper into another world. Not America, and not Russia either, but the world of Yuri's exile.

"Do it. Please. I need your help."

I sit back down at the table and start unpinning and re-pinning each item while he watches, a cigarette dangling from his lips. When I am done with the first tray, I put the cloth down and push my chair away, but he points to the whole stack. There must be about a dozen trays. I look at him for an instant, thinking he must be joking, but his

85

face has hardened into a mask, with that insolent look that makes my heart beat faster. I pick up the next tray. I lose myself in each miniature: a miracle fish glowing with gold rays, a team of horses galloping through the steppes, an angry, crowned princess brandishing a scepter, the face of an apple-cheeked *babushka*.

A few pairs of pale amber earrings and necklaces in creamy yellow and pale brown pinned on another tray catch my eyes. "They are so pretty, I'd love to have one of those."

His eyes turn suspicious, as if I had just revealed a gold digger's nefarious intentions. "You think I am going to give you one?"

"I just think they're lovely, that's all. I'll buy one from you," I add testily, getting up from my chair.

"Finish," he orders with his taskmaster's voice, gripping my arm and holding me down.

I pull my arm out of his grip, stare at him for a moment, my heart pounding with fear and excitement, and pick up the cloth. He keeps an eye on me until I am all done, then checks with his finger to make sure the brooches are spotless.

"Good. Next time you come with me to fair and help out."

"I might not be good for business. I'd ruin your image of sexy Russian stud."

His face breaks into a sly smile before delivering his condescending "smart woman."

I start to get up again but he moves faster than me. He bends me over the kitchen table with an iron hand and penetrates me in one quick move, in the middle of all the jewelry trays.

## 4

November. The Belt Parkway again, the Verrazano-Narrows Bridge arching in my rear-view mirror over a sea of lead, the horizon lost in a soupy fog, not yet the crystal clarity of winter. I am traveling further this time, past Sebastopol, past Yalta, past Kerch, over to the Caucasus, into Georgia. I leave Crimea and the Black Sea for the Sea of Azov. Yuri has invited me for Thanksgiving at a friend's house somewhere between Brighton Beach and Sheepshead Bay. Since David is gone, Thanksgiving means nothing to me but a quiet afternoon while Lulu spends the holiday with her dad, so a Russian Thanksgiving sounds intriguing. It takes me forever to find the house. Outside of Manhattan the streets and avenues become terraces, places and courts, and cross at sharp angles in increasingly odd permutations of numbers and names without any apparent logic, a spiraling maze siphoning me deep into some subterranean world. I recognize the restaurant Ludy's where I had gone with David long ago—vague memory of a huge, half-empty, cavernous hall; of the fishing boats bobbing along the canal; of the seafood restaurant in Manhattan Beach where he had taken me for my birthday to announce it was over between us, but without mentioning he had fallen in love with another woman.

The house appears at the end of a dead-end street, a two-story wood-frame hunched up behind a huge tree, whose tentacle-like roots reach so deep into the yard they look like they are about to choke the house. Yuri is waiting for me at the gate, wearing the slacks he had on my first time in Brooklyn, a good brown shirt, his dressy, lace-up shoes and a navy blue parka.

The old lady who opens the door is the very portrait of the *babushkas* hand-painted on Yuri's brooches: an apple-round face, a brightly colored kerchief tied at the nape of her neck, and a blue apron around her hips. With a smile missing a good amount of teeth, she spills out an incomprehensible flow of Russian, which still manages to make me feel welcome. Yuri grabs her by the waist and twirls her around and around. She bursts into great, savage laughter, punching him in the arm. A woman about my age appears right behind her. Long skirt, lacy white blouse, slippers. Huge, black, sad-looking eyes, long black tresses streaked with white braided down her back. Yuri introduces her as Zibeyda. They are mother and daughter. Yuri buys "merchandise" from Zibeyda's husband, although right now, "husband on business trip."

Thanksgiving means nothing to them either. Not a trace of turkey or pumpkin in the kitchen, although the table is loaded with salads, cutlets, and stuffed cabbage. Babushka, standing up, keeps refilling our plates, especially Yuri's.

"Yuri vacuum!" She points at his plate and laughs her great, savage laugh with a grandmother's indulgence.

"Yuri giant" Zibeyda lifts her hand way above her head. "Viking. Look at him. Tall, blond," she adds admiringly.

She catches me looking at her—my eyes linger on one side of her chest that seems flatter than the other—and pats her hand below her pale neck, at the edge of her blouse.

"Breast cancer," she whispers, and I notice the tip of a folded handkerchief or the lacy edge of a camisole coyly peeking out of her blouse, covering the missing breast. She watches me with her huge dark eyes, without hiding her obvious curiosity. I steal glances at her too, but less overtly. Her hands are exquisite, delicate with transparent skin and pale lavender veins and impeccably filed oval nails. The skin on her face and neckline has an unlined softness and ripeness as though it hasn't seen the light of day or the sun for years. I notice how lovely her lips are, how elegant the curve of her nose. Yet the impression of darkness that envelops her, and the purple circles under her eyes—perhaps marks of insomnia or illness—pervert her fading beauty and give it a tragic cast.

An open door, off the kitchen, offers a glance of an iron bed mounted high, made even higher by a mound of brightly colored quilts and satiny pillows. Except for the icon hanging over the bed in lieu of a crucifix, the room wouldn't be out of place in one of the farmhouses where my grandparents' relatives used to live in Western France.

"Yura says you have daughter?" Zibeyda asks me. "How old?"

"Eight."

"Next time you bring her."

"Well . . . I don't know. She spends her weekends with her dad. . . ."

"Come on, let's go," Yuri interjects. "We have long way back."

"Wait," Zibeyda says. She disappears upstairs and comes back with an album of photos. I wonder if showing family photos is a kind of Russian ritual, a picture being worth a thousand words, or something. I am wrong, it's not a family photo album, but a scrapbook. A large, black and white studio photo of a beautiful young woman with pale, clear skin, gleaming eyes, and voluptuous black hair, in a ravishing three-quarter profile, occupies the first page.

"I was actress in Baku. Long time ago."

"You?"

She turns toward me with a smile, the sad expression lifting, the mouth curving up seductively, revealing, for a second, a glimpse of her past beauty and glamour.

"She was famous actress," Yuri says. He shoots me a defiant look, as if to show me that he, too, has connections with celebrities, before disappearing to smoke on the balcony.

"I know. I change much," Zibeyda says, lowering her eyes.

Yellowed newspaper clippings and photos are slipped between clear plastic sheets. A young Zibeyda wearing a sultana's veil, or a mini-skirt and square-toed shoes, like the heroine of a Godard movie. In one of the photos a group of people in party clothes stand in front of an old house whose wrought-iron balconies drip with exuberant flowers and vines.

"My house," Zibeyda says. "Baku very beautiful city."

She takes me by the wrist to her bedroom, where an old desktop Dell takes up most of a small table. She points to a manuscript of about fifty pages placed by the keyboard. The top page reads, in English: "My Life," with her name printed below: Zibeyda Mihaïlovna V.

The room smells stuffy, suggesting that the window never gets opened. Zibeyda's bed is neatly done with a dark brown bedspread, and none of the exuberance and lavishness of her mother's bed. Along one wall a flimsy bookcase caves under the weight of heavy-bound volumes. The tiny, austere room makes me think of a nun's cell. What would Zibeyda make of my own study, crammed with magazines and books stacked in staggering piles and the walls covered with Lulu's paintings? She slips her manuscript into a manila envelope and presses the envelope in my hands. "Read. Please."

Through the window I see Yuri on the balcony, a shadow clutching his cell phone, pacing back and forth, his brows knitted. I raise my arm to let him know I want to leave.

Outside, the ocean air slaps us with a gust of iodine. In the light of the rising moon the distorted trees seem predatory. A few more decades and the houses will burst under the pressure of nature from below and collapse in heaps of cinderblocks and presswood. I shiver. Unless a tidal wave engulfs the whole neighborhood first.

"You cold?"

"No. It's Zibeyda. I felt oppressed in her room. It's like she's shut herself off from the world."

"A lot of ex-Soviet refugees do that, old ones. I know guy, he was teaching mathematics at University in Saint Petersburg, and now he lives in one-room apartment over Ocean Parkway and he cleans buildings, you know, sweep, mop floor, take out garbage, things like that."

91

"And he's happy here?"

"Happy?" He brays with laughter as if the very notion of happiness were hilarious—another idiotic American concept. "Wife just died, but he says he likes it here. I used to see him sometimes on boardwalk, smoking cigarette, or playing chess with guy from Odessa."

I think of the couples I had seen my first morning in Brighton Beach, strolling on the promenade, dressed in furs coats and hats, frozen in time and space.

"Is it because he's freer here?"

"Maybe, but I don't think he was having problems over there. He had big apartment and everything. America was forbidden dream. So the more you dream of something you can't have, it gets bigger and bigger in your head."

"But it could turn into the opposite, you could be disappointed."

"Correct. Guy told me before he came he thought everybody has car in America, but he doesn't have car, he takes subway. But he still sees the way he imagined before in his mind."

"But you're not like that. You criticize everything all the time!"

He laughs his devilish laugh. "Is because I don't buy bullshit."

# 5

Yuri puts his hand on my hand when I am about to click off the sound system. We've just pulled into his driveway after our dinner in Brooklyn. "Leave it on. I want to listen to this." He pops a ZZ Top tape into my stereo and turns up the volume. We listen for a moment to the fast beat. After a few moments, he clicks the tape off and lights up a cigarette.

"The other day, I didn't tell you how mother died." He opens the window a notch to toss the match out. A gust of chilly, wet air blows in. He takes a long drag on the cigarette.

"I was at dacha with grandmother. It was Sunday wintertime. It was snowing, heavy snow, you understand? You couldn't see very well. Mother was late coming back from city. It was long subway ride, changing twice, train, then half-hour walk on ice path. We waited for long time. But after while, grandmother sent me out to look for her."

He takes a deep breath. His profile is lit up by the shaky red tip of his cigarette, moving from his face to the window like a distress signal in the night.

"I walked toward train station, but I couldn't find her. I went to village, and I came back different way, by railroad tracks. Tracks went through little wood, back of dacha." He pulls on his cigarette and lets the smoke slowly mushroom into a cloud. "I saw something dark on tracks, it was hard to see with snow and it was night already. I thought it was dog run over by train, or bag of coal or something fallen off wagon. I was curious, so I walked closer. I was just curious, you understand? You couldn't see very well, so much snow, so I thought no. I always imagined things. But heart was beating hard. When I got real close you couldn't even tell it was person because coat was covering everything, except. . . ." He takes another long drag on his cigarette and pitches it out the window. "There was boot sticking out." His voice breaks. "I ran all the way back to dacha."

I put my hand on his knee. We stay like this for a while, without moving, without talking. A light drizzle falls noiselessly, and mist covers the windshield inside the car.

He lights up another cigarette. "It was snowing at cemetery. Everything white. Snow had buried coffin even before it was in ground." He pinches his cigarette between thumb and index finger and takes a few angry tokes. "Wasn't fair." There's an edge to his voice. Not pain. Rage. "She shouldn't have died so young. She was younger than you are now."

"I'm so sorry. It's awful."

In the moonlight uncovered by shifting clouds, Yuri's profile is so sharply defined, so delicate, he looks like the sweet little boy in the picture, with his pale hair curling on his temples. He awkwardly folds his big body in the narrow space between the gearshift and the steering wheel, and places his head on my lap.

94

"I wish I was your son."

His words hang in the silence for a long time. I run my fingers softly through his hair. Outside the wind is blowing in sharp gusts, hissing in the trees.

"Let's get out," I whisper.

He sits up, crushes his cigarette with his thumb into the ashtray as if to stamp out the pain, and pushes the door open.

We walk across the road and stand under a cluster of trees that protects us from the drizzle. He wraps his arms around me. The headlights of the rare cars passing by diffuse the rain into an eerie light. "I wish I had been in love with a girl when I was twenty," he says. A feeling passes through me, fluttering like the ghost of lost love, and vanishes in the rain.

It's very late, that night, or perhaps the following night. The nights blend in my memory. He's sitting on his big swivel chair, and me on the floor, leaning against him. A videotape of Vusotsky plays on the VCR. He whispers in Russian. "*Ya tebya lioubliou*." The words come out a little slurred, they lose themselves in Vusotksy's voice. *I love you*. Did I hear that right? I'm not sure. My Russian is shaky. He has been drinking. It's just a mood he's in, I think. Or is it? I say nothing. The same ghost of a feeling passes through me. A memory that I can no longer grasp. I cannot imagine saying those words again. We remain silent, my head on his lap, my arms around his legs.

The syrupy-screeching sounds of violins wake me up later. We're in bed now. I open my eyes to the blurry vision of a tall, blond woman wearing a flowery, half-opened negligee and blood-red nails lying on a fur rug and sticking two fingers in the opening of her panties. A porn tape. Without my glasses, everything looks like an impressionist painting. Squinting hard, I manage to make out images of erect penises entering moist pussies, fading out into exotic flowers opening and closing their petals. With its soft-focus shots, the porn vaguely looks like the psychedelic Pink Floyd tape we watched in Brighton Beach, except with worse music. Yuri mumbles something I don't catch, while I drift in and out of sleep, hypnotized by the kitschy pattern of fade-ins and fade-outs.

"What?"

"I shouldn't watch that crap." He abruptly clicks off the remote. "It's sick." He slips his hand between my legs, teases me for a moment with his fingers, then whispers, "I want to suck your cunt. Go wash yourself." In his taskmaster's voice.

I sit up, fully awake.

"What?"

"I want you clean."

What now? Is it another one of his obsessions? Like taking three showers a day and picking up any piece of clothing that's fallen on the floor with an air of disgust as if it were contaminated?

"I took a shower in the morning."

He nudges me with his elbow.

"Don't argue. Do it."

It's the tone of his voice that turns me on. As though the humiliation, to be sent back to the bathroom to wash up like a child who came to the table with dirty hands, was in itself exciting. I stumble in the dark toward the bathroom and wash myself at the sink. Still, isn't that obsession with cleanliness a sign of distaste for the woman body—or of an obsessive-compulsive disorder, I wonder, while I busy myself splashing water over my legs until all traces of soap are washed off, pat myself dry and stumble back to the bedroom.

"Are you clean?" The callousness of his voice arises in me simultaneous flares of anger and desire. He tastes me with the tip of his tongue to make sure, then attacks me voraciously with his tongue and lips as though releasing a pent-up rage, and fires me up to a crescendo of tension so intense my body can't resist anymore and explodes in a violent orgasm that leaves me shaking from head to toe—like a guitar cord so taut it starts vibrating before snapping.

The next day. He's sitting at his desk. Bills and invoices are stacked on his left and he is entering lists of sold items on a ledger with his small, fastidious handwriting. I am lying on the Louis XV sofa, Zibeyda's manuscript open on my lap. The ceiling light is turned on because it's too dark to see properly. We each have a mug of steaming tea. This moment of intimate domesticity with Yuri is unnerving. I look at his massive back slumped over his desk, his handsome feet in his Adidas slippers, with a mix of tenderness and malaise. To avoid it I start reading Zibeyda's pages. The book is taking place in Baku in the sixties, in the heyday of Azerbaijan's movie industry. It's about a beautiful, young, aspiring actress with a sweep of jet-black hair and smoldering eyes, who catches the attention of a dashing KGB officer. But she is in love with an Armenian movie director, famous for making stars out of young starlets, and she rejects the KGB officer. That's in the first ten pages. The style is awkward at times—it's obvious that the author's native tongue isn't English—but the story has elements of a romantic saga, witty and exuberant, in a middle-eastern vein.

Without turning toward me Yuri asks in a dubious voice, "Is good?"

"It's entertaining."

"Can you help her?"

"Help her how?"

"Get published."

"She only asked me to read it."

"Well that's what she wants." His voice rises. "Why you think she gave it to you? Can you help her?"

How could I have been so naive? Of course the dinner was arranged so that Zibeyda would give me her manuscript in the hope I would put her in touch with an editor. No wonder I had such an urge to escape when she handed it to me. I slip the pages back into the folder on the floor. "I don't know." I try to keep my voice as neutral as possible.

He swivels on his big chair to face me and presses on. "What do you mean, you don't know?"

"I've only read a few pages, and her English isn't that good. . . . She'd have to work with someone, an editor or a writer. No agent or publisher would take on a manuscript that needs that much work."

"Could you work with her?"

I immediately regret having even suggested that. Anything I will say from this point on will be used against me later: "You said, You promised, You told me."

"It's a big job to do that. I wouldn't have the time

now. I am working on my own novel. Anyway, I'll tell you what I think when I've read all the pages."

I can see in his eyes that he thinks that's a lame excuse. I have access to publishers. I am a published writer myself. All I have to do is snap my fingers and things will happen.

# 6

December. I haven't told Yuri anything about my Christmas plans—the sparkling tree, the presents tied in silver and gold ribbons, the big Christmas Eve dinner party with our friends, the table set with my grandmother's sterling silverware, the candles, the champagne, the *foie gras* brought from France by my mother, the elaborate *bûche de Noël* bought at the best French pastry shop in town. I've only told him my mother was coming to visit, as she does every year. He hasn't asked either. He is busy with his fairs—the few weeks before Christmas are crucial for vendors, as they often make most of their money for the whole year at that time. Still, I feel guilty to be throwing a party while he will work late that night and sleep alone in a motel, even though I know very well that even if he were home alone I couldn't bring myself to invite him.

On Christmas' Eve, when we are already all sitting at the table, my mother makes her entrance down the staircase in her usual, grand manner, her black velvet skirt sweeping the steps and a pair of pearl and gold earrings I have given her at a previous Christmas glowing at her ears. She looks surly. Is it about the chocolate truffles she didn't have time to roll in cacao powder? Or about Lulu talking back to her or ignoring her? She sits at the head of the table, where David used to sit, opposite me. So she's finally succeeded in running him off! After all their epic fights, like that time when she pursued him with a wooden spoon and he jumped on our bed to escape her, all the banged doors, the teary reconciliations, he's gone, and we are back where we started, mother-daughter face to face without a man.

We all raise our flutes to wish my mother happy holidays. She regally accepts our toasts, but her smiles are confined to her end of the table.

"Unfortunately I will be alone after the New Year." She's spoken loud enough for me to hear her from the other end of the table. Her neighbor, a British novelist whose work she admires, nods with sympathy. She glances toward me. My stomach clutches. Of course that's the reason for her anger. She usually stays until mid-January. But this time, for the first time, I have changed the plans. I have an assignment for a woman's magazine, an interview of Jeanne Moreau, and I'm taking Lulu with me to spend the first week of January in Paris, so my mother will fly back to Finland, where she spends her winters, before we come back.

"They are abandoning me." She points with her chin in my direction when she is sure to have caught my eyes. Then, while I pass around the plates with the *bûche de Noël*, she stands up and announces she's tired. She waves like a star departing before the end of the festivities, and the black velvet skirt sweeps up the stairs accompanied by a chorus of goodnights.

I raise my flute and drain it bottoms up as if it were vodka.

Christmas morning. My mother has fallen asleep on the couch, her shoulders wrapped in the cashmere scarf I've given her. Her head tilted back, her mouth open, she's snoring softly. Lulu is sitting under the tree, surrounded by a tangle of wrinkled tissue paper and coiled ribbons, listening to the new CD player Santa Claus has brought her, headphones plugged to her ears. The snow, which has fallen during the night, bathes the living room in a pale, translucent glow. Scattered around the coffee table, among the remnants of our breakfast, the presents have turned into a puny pile of pretty objects whose magic fairy dust evaporated when they were released from their wrappings.

It is ten thirty AM and we're already done with Christmas.

I call Yuri to wish him Merry Christmas, even though I know he doesn't celebrate it.

"I want to see you, " he says in a sleepy voice.

My mother's legs are stretched on the couch, her naked feet stick out of her nightgown. The toes are twisted like the stubby roots of a tree, overlapping one another. The big toenail is thick and discolored. Her feet have started to look like my grandfather's feet, gnarled and uncared-for—the feet of an old man. With a pang I wonder if my feet will look like hers at her age. I remember the delicate stilettos she used to wear, and how, when we would visit my aunt and uncle on Avenue de Versailles in Paris, my aunt would ask her to remove them to protect the parquet.

"Are you still there?" Yuri's voice seems to travel from a great distance.

I don't know where I am. My head is throbbing as if

it were stuffed with cloth. Not enough sleep. Too much Champagne.

"Yeah. . . ." My voice is white, nearly inaudible.

"Get into your car and come over."

I have a vision of the Garden State, blindingly white, the tires of the Saab biting two smooth curves into the fresh powder, the wipers lazily swatting at fat flakes floating in the cottony air, Pink Martini on the stereo.

"I can't. It's Christmas."

"Oh." His voice is muffled as though he is going back to sleep. "Call me when Christmas is over."

As the date of our departure for Paris approaches, my mother becomes more uptight. She gets ready even later than usual when we plan to go out, or silently leafs through magazines on the couch as though she were in a doctor's waiting room. If Lulu refuses to read a French book with her, my mother storms out of her room and bangs the door. On New Year's Eve we drink Champagne again and eat oysters, but I can see my mother's eyes cloud with tears when we go to bed.

In the afternoon of New Year's Day, a black town car pulls up to drive Lulu and me to JFK. My mother comes down to say goodbye. She has slipped her Persian lamb coat over her nightgown and wrapped her new cashmere scarf around her shoulders. Lulu hugs her and hops into the car. The snow has hardened on the sidewalk into a slippery film.

My mother's kisses fall on my cheeks like hard little pellets. Her eyes have that liquid look of despair that makes them look greener. "I didn't want to be the one left behind," she says. Her voice is trembling, maybe from the cold. I wrap the scarf another loop around her neck and press her against me as hard as I can.

Lulu hangs her head at the window. *"Tu viens, Maman?"*

My mother's body feels slight. Her flesh seems to have melted, her muscular shoulders bonier than they used to be. She was always the one leaving on summer vacations and weekends, rushing to her "other life," while I lived with my grandparents.

I close the door to the cab and turn to wave at her through the back windshield, thrilled at being the one who leaves, for once, instead of being left. We are bonded so tightly, each on one end of a seesaw, that if I give a good kick to propel myself upward, she will automatically plunge down, and vice-versa. I am still a part of her, our hearts beating together. She is immobile like a white statue against the white snow, with her white fur coat over her white nightgown, her feet in furry slippers, her white hair still spiked from the night, tightening the white scarf around her neck. Alone. Vulnerable. Abandoned. My heart sinks. I want to jump out of the car and pick her up in my arms. Little Marinette with the big bow in her hair and the radiant smile at the wheel of my grandfather's Duesenberg roadster, the picture I have on my shelf next to one of Lulu's at the same age—four. But the cab, skidding slightly on the snow that hasn't been plowed, has already turned the corner and I can't see her anymore. Lulu clamps her earphones on and we speed toward Houston Street, toward JFK, toward the plane that will set us free.

# 7

The first message on my voicemail, when we stand at the immigration line, back from Paris, on January 8, is from Yuri.

"Are you back yet? Call me."

Two days later I am on my way to New Jersey. In Paris I was too busy seeing my friends and working on my article to think much about him, but as soon as I set foot at JFK, I craved seeing him, as if he was the sole reason I was back in New York. The snow has melted. In spite of the white webs still caught in the trees, making them look like Christmas trees, the Garden State is gray and dry. I turn up the heat and put Pink Martini on, humming the lyrics off-key, floating into the old, familiar dream.

I've brought him a set of sheets, as well as some pots and pans and some 1940s horn-handled silverware from my apartment, which he looks at with disdain when I unpack them.

"What's that old crap?" he says.

"It's not old crap," I correct him. "They are vintage."

He shrugs and prepares another pot of tea, making a show of giving me the yellow mug, while he takes the black one, "*Tchernoi kak moi zhizn*—black like my life."

I am unnerved by his dark mood. We have left Chekhov's melancholy territory and entered Dostoevsky's bleak *Notes from the Underground*. Before Christmas, Yuri had been his usual self, mischievous and provocative. But I wasn't prepared for his diatribe about America. Not the America for which he had had a violent passion, mainly expressed through a longing for Levi's jeans and American women, but the America that has become an obstacle to his dreams. He wanted to become the next Willy Loman, the best salesman in America, make millions. How can he do that without legal papers? He is condemned to sell his "Russian crap" at crafts fair where he can pass unnoticed. There was good money in the first years, when customers were still fascinated with Soviet souvenirs, but they are already moving on to other, more current merchandise. Plus, the constant driving is exhausting. No matter which way he turns, the obstacles are insurmountable. It's unfair that the only way he can get status is by marrying US citizen.

His bitterness unsettles me. For the first time since I've met him I wonder if his anger might be directed at me.

Night. Yuri is standing naked over me. He whips his leather belt off the waistband of his jeans. Cracks it like a riding switch, his rage spilling over into sex.

"No." I raise my hand in defense. "Not that."

Reluctant, he drops the belt. "You must learn how to take pain. Like yoga. Breathe past pain."

My hand remains raised like that of a cop stopping traffic. I look into his eyes, challenging him. "Only when I feel like it."

He shrugs and takes out a toolbox of toys I've never seen. Shiny, bright plastic. He pulls one out, a royal blue dildo. A majestic, but peaceful color, blue. It's bigger than his own member, the tip tooled to represent thick recesses of skin. It excites me more than the belt.

"I want to do it there," he says, fingering my anus. Have you ever done it?"

"Yes," I breathe, "long time ago."

"And this," he holds the blue dildo in the light of his clip lamp like a candle, "in front at the same time, OK?"

"OK," I whisper.

"Together, OK?"

"OK, but gently."

He laughs his devilish laugh.

"Of course."

The rolled *r* "of course" doesn't bode well. But he enters me with unexpected gentleness, and miraculously, there's hardly any resistance. I push past the pain like he said. I trust him when it comes to sex. He knows what he's doing. The sensation of being entirely filled, full beyond desire, is irresistible. I collapse under him in a long, delicious sigh. He, on the other hand, rolls off me and drops condom and dildo to the floor with a disgusted flip of his wrist. His mouth is pursed in a dubious arc.

"Is OK. . . ." he says, "but I don't like so much."

Morning. Yuri's angry mood has evaporated like dew under the sun. It has snowed a little during the night. He carries my bag to my car, wipes off the windshields and windows with the stiff bristle brush I keep in the trunk, and when he's made sure every glass surface is clean for the road, he runs a finger over my lips.

"You're like bird," he says with a sad smile. "When you leave, you forget everything."

On the Garden State, on the way back, the sun is radiant, pearls of snow glitter in the outstretched arms of the pine trees. The sky is brilliant blue. Life doesn't have a crease. When I pull out of the Holland Tunnel, my cell phone rings. It's him.

"I just wanted to make sure you got back safely," he says.

## 8

January. "Do you mind if I sit next to you?" I look up from the *Book Review*, which I have been reading while waiting for Lulu's club routine. Bill. He's got a crooked smile and a loose strand of hair falling on his forehead, which gives him a charming, boyish look. My heart gives a little bounce but I put my index finger across my lips because Lulu is up.

She's been practicing all week to get the hang of the wrist movement, tossing the clubs upward while doing a somersault, then catching them on the fly—all with the deftness of a juggler. But this time, just as she springs up from her last somersault, one of the clubs, instead of twirling gracefully, slips out of her hand and lands by the judges' table. A foul. She scrambles to pick it up, rises on tiptoe for her final salute, and beats a stiff retreat behind the curtain. She reappears on the bleachers a moment later and collapses, her head in my lap, hiccuping with sobs. Her goal was to make the national meet in Chicago in a few weeks, but this blunder will have cost her the chance. I console her until she dries her eyes and runs back to the practice room.

"Your daughter seemed really upset."

Bill moves a little closer to me on the bench. He's

wearing baggy jeans and a navy blue sweater, and, annoyingly, his clean-cut, preppy look still stirs up a wave of desire in me.

"Yes. She works so hard, but . . . I don't think she'll ever become a competitive gymnast. Oh well . . . that's not the point. It's a good discipline."

"Same with my daughter. We won't see them at the Olympics."

I glance at him. "So . . . you're back from the West Coast?"

"For the time being, yes." He motions to the door with his chin. "Would you care for a cup of coffee? Come, I'll buy you one."

It's a joke, considering how bad and cheap the coffee is at the meets. I hesitate, but I'm off the hook until Lulu does Hoops.

"OK."

We carry our plastic cups to the backyard. It's cold but sunny and we sit on a wooden bench facing a group of silver clapboard houses surrounded by lawns and majestic trees. In contrast to the anonymous and institutional-looking schools, where most of the meets take place, this is a lovely, intimate private school on an old Massachusetts estate.

"Nice school," he says cautiously, throwing glances around him.

"Jackie Kennedy was a student here, they say."

"Really?"

I shrug. "Maybe it's just a rumor."

He stretches one arm behind me on the bench and I close my eyes for a moment, letting myself slip into my old fantasy. It's short-lived. A few seconds later, Bill opens the afternoon's program. His finger runs down the list of names. Ribbons. Hoops. Balls. Clubs.

"Oops! My daughter's up now. I should go in."

It's a two-day meet, and we are all spending the night at the Howard Johnson a few miles up the road. After dinner, one of the mothers suggests meeting at the bar after the girls are asleep, and Bill and I go up in the same elevator—the two girls shyly giggling at each other without a word. Even though they are on the same team, they are two grades apart and they might as well belong on different planets. I put Ludivine to bed, then touch up my makeup and take the elevator back down. In the sinister bar, half a dozen local men in various stages of obesity and inebriety are watching a hockey game blaring from four TV monitors hung high, the rumbling of the announcer's voice punctuated by the dull thump of the puck. Frigid A/C blows on top of the heating system, inexplicably. No trace of Bill. Alba is sitting with Anna, the coach, and two other mothers, all of them divorced, huddled around glasses of wine and beer bottles, laughing loudly. They call me over, but I am in no mood for another divorced women's evening. I know them too well. I decide to head back upstairs, and just as I am standing in front of the elevators, Bill walks out. He dances a little comical two-step in his sneakers accompanied by arched eyebrows when he sees me.

"What are you up to? Going to sleep already? How about a drink? Too damn depressing here!"

I laugh, relieved to see him. "You should see the bar!"

The lonely guys in baseball caps screwed backwards are still perched on their stools like chubby herons. Alba and the others wave at us, but we sit side by side on a banquette away from the bar, our back to the TVs.

"Hope you're not a hockey fan?"

He orders a Pilsner and I a glass of red wine, even though I already know, from having tasted it at dinner, that it's heavy and sour. By the time he has ordered a second, then a third beer, and I am starting on my second glass of wine, he has vented about his wife, "not ex yet," and told me she is moving back to San Francisco with the kids and that he has no choice but to move there too. "Although I might be bi-coastal for a while." His sidelong glance revs up my hopes. "Sorry to be ranting." Every time he picks up his glass, the sleeve of his dark blue sweater brushes against my forearm and a quiver of desire ripples through me. He stretches his right arm on the back of the banquette, like he had done earlier on the bench, his fingers grazing my shoulder, but just the tips, as if he didn't want to commit to the full hand.

"How about going out for a walk?"

It's all asphalt around the hotel and a little bit of frosted grass along the driveways, and more frosted grass on a hill sloping up to the Howard Johnson sign, rising like a crucifix on the Golgotha. We circle it and find a spot at the back, with a view of the strip-mall, a sight so dismal that when he takes me in his arms, my fantasy about him collapses in avid, raunchy desire. To hell with old-fashioned courting going nowhere. To hell with relationships. It's clear Bill is just a new divorcé cut loose and drunk on his new freedom just as I am. He presses me

112

against the sign and kisses me greedily. Then he unbuttons my coat and slips his hand between my thighs.

"I want to take you," he pants, "right now." He fumbles with my zipper and I let him pull it down. "Right here."

My breath comes out heavy and shallow and I wriggle out of my pants to give him more room. But after we have feverishly groped each other for a few minutes, he disentangles himself and zips my pants back up.

"We should go in," he says. "We wouldn't want to be caught like this with our daughters in the hotel, now, would we?"

I want to slap him for being a tease; what do they call men like that, *cunt-teasers*? But what exactly did I want? We are on the same boat, he and I, like aging sixteen-year-olds fooling around in their parents' backyard. He takes my hand to bring me to my feet. From under his loose strands of hair, he shoots me a smile conveying naughtiness and guilt—but whether he feels guilty for having made out with me outside the Howard Johnson while on duty with his daughter, or for abruptly interrupting our making-out session, I have no idea. He gives me a chaste peck on the cheek in the elevator when we get to his floor and a military salute with his hand.

Overwhelmed by a gloomy mood, I sit on the toilet in the dark. If only I could be in a Super 8 Motel with Yuri, under a puke-green bedspread! I flip my cell phone and dial his number, which goes straight to voicemail. I take a hot shower, then change into clean underwear and a T-shirt, rub moisturizer on my face, and lie down on my back under the blanket, Ludivine's little body coiled like a cat inside my arms.

# 1

February. The rhythmic competition is in New Jersey, two exits away from Yuri's place, as I realize on the way down this morning. On the Brahms Sonata Adagio, Lulu has done a near-perfect routine, her glittery, turquoise hoop victoriously suspended in her overstretched hands for the final salute. She struts off the mat in the rigid regulation posture while the girls on her team, crowded at the auditorium entrance, give her a loud ovation. I stand up to applaud and scream "Bravo!" Corina's mother, Alba, who has come with us, stands up too and yells "Bravo, Bravo!" We clap our hands until Lulu disappears behind the curtain. When the applause dies down, I sneak out to the lobby, and, without pausing to think, dial Yuri's number. He answers on the first ring.

"Guess what. I'm in Cherry Hill."

"What?"

"I'm here the whole day. Lulu's got a competition. Want to come over?"

I quickly give him directions. No sooner have I hung up, than I regret my phone call. What a terrible idea to invite him to meet me at the school, I must have been looking for trouble. Beads of sweat drip down from my armpits. My cheeks burn. I walk to the back door and step out into the cold air. There is a pile of plastic chairs stacked up at one end of the deck and a soda machine. Stupid impulse. I have tried so hard to keep him away from Lulu. And now this. I am getting more and more confused about Yuri, given to twisted rationalizations like this: if I'm not willing to break up with him, then I should admit that we have a "relationship." Besides, compared with Bill's evasive, almost loutish behavior the weekend before, isn't Yuri shining with steadfastness and . . . *hoooonesty*? Isn't the wall with which I am protecting myself a sign of class snobbishness and paranoia?

After my phone call I keep walking out of the auditorium and checking the parking lot. If I can intercept him before he walks into the school, I will limit the risk of Lulu running into him, but after an hour or so I give up waiting and settle down on my bench and watch Lulu do her club routine. I figure he has gone back to sleep. But just as Lulu takes her salute, I glance toward the door of the auditorium and I see him hovering, hesitant to come in. My heart leaps into my throat. Huge, with his long black leather coat and his pale hair slicked back, he looks incongruous and slightly menacing among the delicate gymnasts, the solid middle-class parents and the coaches. A dark scenario unfolds in my mind, in which someone will notice he doesn't belong and will try to throw him out; he will defend himself with a few well-placed jabs and then someone else will call the cops. I wave at him and with my index finger signal him to wait for me outside. He frowns and stays at the door. I lean towards Alba. Since the night we have tried to drink Yuri's Moldavian wine, I have mentioned him to her a couple of times. He sounds exotic and intriguing when I talk about him, but to be confronted with him marching in with his big black leather coat, and a surly look in his pale eyes as though he were ready to punch you in the jaw if you look at him the wrong way, is another thing altogether. Alba is reading *The New York Times Magazine*. There are still three girls to go before Corina.

"I am stepping out for a little while," I whisper. "I have to say hi to a friend." She turns her head toward the door. I hope she doesn't see the friend I am talking about.

He is waiting for me on the back porch. I see him through the glass door, pacing and smoking a cigarette. His face cracks into a tight smile when he sees me, but he looks nervous and ill at ease. "What are you doing here?"

"Lulu has a competition. Rhythmic gymnastics? Remember?"

He flips his cigarette in the grass and looks over his shoulder with shifty eyes as if he's expecting someone to come and get him. The INS? The FBI? The KGB? The FSB? The MVD?

"Can you leave?" His lips hardly move. His voice is almost inaudible.

I nod.

We are like co-conspirators planning a dirty trick.

"Let's go. Meet me at van. I am parked up front. Do you have time to go to my place?"

I go back in to pick up my coat and my bag. Alba's eyebrows go up but she doesn't say anything.

"I have to step out for a bit. Would you mind . . . if Lulu does her ribbon routine before I come back? Can you tell her? I won't be long."

119

She gives me an ambiguous look, which I choose to believe is a look of complicity, but doesn't ask any questions.

"Take your time," she says. "I'm not going anywhere. If you miss her routine, I'll tell her. No big deal."

The van is parked in the front lot, in full view of the school, and he's sitting behind the wheel, his door open. When I lean in, he pushes my head down into the crotch of his unzipped pants.

I pull back and push him away. "Not here! Are you crazy! Not in front of the school."

He grins as if it were the wittiest joke. I walk around, shaking my head like a disapproving schoolmarm and climb in through the passenger door, which I make sure to bang to show my displeasure. He zips up his pants and puts his hand on mine and searches my eyes to see if I am still angry. I am not really. It's another one of his schoolboy pranks.

How strange to find myself in his apartment in the middle of a day I am spending with Lulu, and alarming, too, as both my lives are dangerously converging. He drags me to his room and we fall on the bed.

"How much time you have?"

The ribbon routine! It has taken us more than half an hour to get to his place. I'll never make it back on time. I close my eyes. He pulls my pants down without taking them off all the way and enters me. I grab the wooden headboard of the bed with both my hands and surrender under the weight of this gesticulating giant. The teakettle whistles in the kitchen, forgotten. He lets out a curse and gets up to turn it off while I drift into a half sleep. Even though it's hardly past lunchtime, the contours of the bedroom, whose small window is obscured by a bush, are dissolving into shadows and I sink into the bed, my own boundaries melting. I hardly feel the texture of the sheet or the weight of the sleeping bag over me.

"You asleep?" Yuri sits near me and hands me a steaming cup of tea.

I jump up and look at my watch.

"Oh my God we have to go."

"OK, OK. Drink first. Then I drive you back."

At the school he gets out of the van with me. I would have preferred if he had just dropped me off, but I don't have the heart to refuse him a cup of coffee. As soon as we walk in, I know I've made a mistake. A swarm of girls in shimmering leotards is crowding the buffet set up in the lobby, devouring muffins and packs of chips. A few of them glance up and move to the side to make room for him. Alba is coming out of the auditorium and walks toward us. I've missed Lulu's ribbon routine. My heart beating, I wonder if I've missed the next one—which was it? Hoops? Balls? Who knows? Everything has become a blur. I feel dizzy and lean against the buffet table to keep my balance. Next to me, Yuri is paying for his coffee and flirting with the teenage girl who's handing him his change.

Noticing my confusion, Alba puts her hand on my arm to reassure me. "Don't worry. You missed Ribbons, but she's fine. I told her you'd be back soon. Balls are starting in a little while."

Yuri turns to her and watches her attentively, perhaps noticing her Brazilian accent. Or maybe she is to his taste. Alba is petite, pretty, with a mass of tightly curled black hair.

"Yuri, Alba," I introduce them.

She looks at him with curiosity and holds out her hand. It wouldn't have been hard to connect him with the Moldavian wine and my weekend in Brighton Beach.

"Alba is from Brazil," I say, as if we're about to have a normal conversation.

Yuri's face beams.

"Brazil? Is my dream. I hear Brazilian girls are goooorgeous. With long dark hair." He makes a gesture with his hand to evoke a long mane cascading down his back, the same gesture he had done when he had talked about Tasha and about Catherine Zeta-Jones. "As soon as I get papers I go there."

I am mortified—not so much humiliated as ashamed, like the mother of a badly behaved son. Alba glances at me with consternation. I try to change the subject, but he won't let it go.

"What's the best beach in Rio?"

"Ipanema," Alba says, keeping her voice as neutral as possible.

Lulu and Corina bounce out of the auditorium at that moment, and jump up and down at the buffet table, repeating and copying each other: "Mom, can I have a muffin, Mom can I have a muffin, Mom can I have a muffin?" until one of us pays attention. I get them each a muffin and a banana to distract them, but while I am paying, I hear Yuri insist behind my back.

"Is that true, what they say about Brazilian girls?"

I am dying. Will he just shut up already.

When I turn around, Alba's face has remained impassible. Bless her.

"There are all kinds." She takes a step back, pulls her fur coat over her shoulders, with the air of wanting to distance herself from the conversation as much as possible, and nods a goodbye.

I take Yuri by the arm and pull him away.

"My daughter is going to compete soon. I have to go in and watch her."

"OK, OK. I go." He puts his coffee cup down and lifts the collar of his leather coat. I walk him to the door. For a moment he struggles with the wind outside, the flaps of his coat beating against his calves, his tall body rigid as if he were bracing himself against a powerful storm but can't quite manage it. When he gets to his van, he turns around and waves in my direction. I move my fingers feebly against the pane of glass.

"*Who was he?*" Lulu asks when I get back to the buffet table. "He was *weird*." The girls giggle and make faces at each other.

I am appalled by Yuri's embarrassing questions about Brazilian girls, and even more appalled to have let Lulu see him. A scene with my mother comes back to me. I had gone back to France for the summer. She was cooking a barbecue in my grandparents' garden, and she had received my cousins naked, with only an apron tied over her breasts and thighs, entirely exposing her backside, "because it was so hot." Instead of being angry, I had been filled with shame.

"He's *different*," I tell Lulu, using the politically correct American answer destined to smooth out potential prejudices against foreigners. "Do you girls want some chili?"

They burst into laughter. "Mom, we just had a muffin!" and run back in. I buy a regular coffee with milk and sip it alone in the lobby, then stroll back in and sit down next to Alba. She shoots me a look of complicity mixed with commiseration. I content myself with a vague smile and bury myself in the *Sunday Times*.

## 2

At first I don't pay attention when Yuri mentions "the virgin." It might be the same inattention that made me overlook his mention of the *goooorgeous* woman who turned out to be Tasha, his now ex-wife. Yuri is quite a talker. For a couple of hours every other night, he calls on his cell phone from the highway, alone like a truck driver, his radio playing softly in the background, and I half-listen to him talking, lulled by his stream of consciousness, Lulu asleep in the next room. I can never remember the girl's name. Mostly he calls her the "virgin," for obvious reasons. It's been a long time since he's stopped talking about his marriage plans. It's a relief not to hear him rant and rave about this or that woman, and how they are all bitches out to get him, and how he needs to have his papers so that he can leave and go to Moscow, and not feel like a prisoner anymore, waiting for the hour of his liberation. So when the "virgin" starts coming up in his nightly talks, I figure she is a friend. An American girl from Maryland, whose parents own a farm in the boonies.

It's only after a few weeks that I realize, not only has he developed a relationship with the virgin, but he's considering marrying her. After being burned once by his first Russian fiancée——the one for whom he bought the Louis XV set of furniture—and a second time by Tasha, he figures that a simple American girl might be best. It won't be a fake marriage, or a love marriage this time, but rather an old-fashioned marriage of convenience. The virgin is twenty-three, has a clerical job in Baltimore, a pleasant personality, a "good body" but an "ugly face." He has met the family, has been invited to dinner, brought them presents, but—he tells me—he can't resolve to sleep with her. "I can't fuck her," he whines. "She doesn't turn me on. She thinks I am gay!" According to him, he occasionally spends the night in her apartment and they just engage in tepid fooling around.

While every mention of Tasha makes my stomach tighten in an ugly knot as I imagine them in the steamiest poses, I feel no jealousy toward the virgin, since Yuri doesn't desire her. In fact, she relieves me from a weight, especially from those dark moods that he gets into lately when his future seems blocked. She could provide the perfect foil if they got married: he would get his papers, a home with a wife, and we might even still have our sexual encounters. A secret affair. Excited by the idea, I encourage him to go ahead with the marriage and finally get his "status."

It's around that time that I give Yuri the dates of my trip to Vietnam: the last week of March and the first two weeks of April, before the monsoon season starts. As usual when I am about to leave the States, his mood turns sour, as it reminds him that he cannot travel. Even though I suspect his sulkiness is meant to make me feel guilty, I sympathize with his frustration. So when he asks me if he could stay at my place for a couple of days before I leave, while he takes care of "business" in Brooklyn, I accept in order to soften the blow, but not without trepidation: it will be the first time he will come over while Lulu is at home.

"You need to arrive after ten PM, OK? After Lulu goes to sleep. And there's a rhythmic gymnastics meet that weekend, so we'll have to leave early on Saturday."

"I'm here." Yuri's voice on the phone startles me awake. It's two AM. I asked him to come after Lulu's bedtime, but I didn't expect he would arrive so late. I've fallen asleep all dressed on my bed. "Right in front of door. At fire hydrant. Come down and help me out."

He's standing by the open trunk of his white Lincoln, surrounded by a staggering pile of boxes and suitcases full of merchandise, which he can't leave in his car for security reasons. Horrified, I can only imagine the noise he will make carrying everything up my five flights of stairs in the middle of the night while I keep guard near his car. Watching him pick up the first case, I think of Willy Loman, his idol, and of the Mongols carting their wares on camelback across the Central Asian steppes. When Lulu wakes up in the morning, she will be confronted with that same pile of merchandise in the apartment, not to mention the fridge overflowing with plastic bags containing red caviar, kielbasa, black bread, cheese, and the flask of Stoli he tucks away in the freezer. This is not quite the way I would have chosen to officially introduce him into our household—actually, I foolishly thought I could hide him from her—but it's too late now. Yuri's shoes are already lined up by the front door and he's padding around in his

Adidas slip-ons, his yoga mat under his arm, looking for a place to levitate on his fist. I quickly usher him into the guestroom, where he will spend the night, and where I briefly join him later.

The next morning, when Lulu gets up, I explain to her that I'm helping out a friend by letting him stay for a couple of nights and she inspects the heap of boxes without comment. I often have French friends staying over, but this is the first time I've brought a lover into my apartment while she is at home, and it seems to me Yuri's boxes are flashing red warning lights. I quickly whisk Lulu off to school and after I return I ask Yuri to come back after she's gone to bed in the evening—but not as late as last night.

On Friday night, when Yuri returns at ten PM on the dot, I remind him that Lulu and I will leave early the next morning for the rhythmic gymnastics meet. He can let himself out later when he wakes up, just pull the door behind him. In the dim light of the guest room I see him tighten his mouth like a sulky child. A surge of guilt fires up another round of twisted logic. Is it fair, just because I deem him socially inappropriate, to banish him from my life? Is it even fair to me? After all, we still have fun moments together, and this weekend is our last chance to see each other for a few weeks. In a new fit of impulsiveness, I offer him to stay the whole weekend until Sunday night. We can all have dinner together when Lulu and I come back. I hand him a set of keys with many repeated recommendations not to lose them, as if I were talking to an irresponsible twelve-year-old.

At five AM, as Lulu and I leave for another ride up the deserted Henry Hudson Highway and the Palisades, the smell of freshly mowed grass wafts through my open window. Dawn on the highway, on an early spring morning, is America at its best, America of the movies, cars flowing by, glittery bumpers, bright divider lines, bushy trees and lawns in crew cuts, America smooth as a dream park where everything is fresh and clean and every bump manicured.

In the evening, I call Yuri from the hotel to see how he is doing in New York, but my call goes straight to voicemail. I figure he must have gone out. After all, why would he stay home alone on a Saturday night?

Sunday. Eleven AM. I call Yuri again on his cell phone, then on my home phone. Still no answer. Panic. What if he has drunk everything in sight at my place? What if he has fallen asleep with a cigarette between his fingers, and the whole building is aflame? I call my home number again half an hour later. If he hears my voice, he might answer the phone. I yell into the answering machine, willing him to answer. "Pick up! Yuri! Pick up!" I repeat it in Russian, hoping the sounds of his native tongue will rouse him from deep slumber. Still nothing.

The day drags on, the competitions follow one another in a predictable and brain-numbing order. I call Yuri at regular intervals. Something is wrong, I know it. How irresponsible of me to have let him stay in the apartment by himself and trusted him with my keys! On the drive back, while Ludivine listens to the Beatles ("love me yeah yeah yeah" and "Yesterday" crackling from her headphones) cataclysmic images erupt in my mind: Yuri passed out on the couch, drunk, clumps of vomit on his chest, or drunk, a cigarette dangling from his fingers, the couch catching fire and going up in flames, or Yuri gone with my keys, concocting to come back one day when I am out to steal my new laptop and my grandmother's sapphire ring. As we ascend the four stories, it's the idea of Lulu finding Yuri naked, drunk on the couch, that alarms me the most. I manage to squeeze in the door before her and I run to the living room— empty!—to my bedroom—empty!—to the guest room—empty! No trace of Yuri anywhere. Not even his Adidas slip-ons. Only the suitcases and trunks still stacked in the hallway signal that he will come back. I don't know whether to feel relieved (no fire, no tragedy, no uncomfortable encounter between a drunk Yuri and Ludivine, sapphire ring still in its case) or even more alarmed: What happened to him?

At seven, just as Lulu is getting out of the bathtub and into her pajamas, my phone rings. It's him.

"I'm coming. I'm round corner. I bring groceries for soup."

A soup? Since when does he cook soups?

Ten minutes later he is at the door, carrying two bulging supermarket bags filled to the brim and a six-pack of beer.

Lulu turns her head from the couch, where she has just settled to watch the preview of the Academy Awards and stares at this blond giant, whom she must remember from the Cherry Hill meet, who has just let himself in with a key and is dropping groceries on the counter as if he were at home. A feeling of nausea grips me, but I embark on a flurry of self-serving justifications. Isn't it better to be up front with one's child? What's wrong with having a man in my life? Granted, Yuri may not be the best candidate for the part, but is that a reason to be ashamed of him?

"Ludivine, this is Yuri." I try to make my voice natural and confident. "Yuri, this is Ludivine. You met, remember, at Cherry Hill? Yuri's going to have dinner with us . . . uh . . . cook dinner for us, actually."

She gives him a tiny half-wave of the hand from the far end of the living room.

"What are you watching?" Yuri asks, marching toward her.

"The Oscars."

He squats next to her for a moment, watches the sweep of ball gowns on the red carpet, the precious stones glittering on the stars' earlobes and necklines, listens to the gossip.

"That's Julia Roberts? I hate her smile. Big mouth. Look at all those teeth."

Lulu shoots him a venomous side look.

"Why are you watching this?" Yuri insists. "It's American . . . Hollywood propaganda."

"Yuri!" I call from the kitchen before he's done more damage.

"I like it," Ludivine answers coldly, stretching her legs under the blanket she likes to wrap herself in to watch TV, announcing the end of the conversation by staring hard and unblinkingly at the screen.

"I tried to call you all day, Yuri," I tell him when he comes back to the kitchen. "Was anything wrong?"

"No, everything fine. I am going to make borscht. Have you ever had?"

With disbelief, I watch him busy himself at the counter, unpacking a pack of beets, a head of cabbage, onions, a bunch of parsley, another one of dill, asking for a large pot. This display of domesticity would warm my heart if I didn't find it so suspicious. Something's wrong, but I can't figure out what yet. When all the vegetables are chopped and the soup's underway, he sits down at the table across from me and pops open a beer.

"Want one?"

I shake my head. "What happened last night, Yuri?"

He takes his time, tastes his beer, pouts. It's a Budweiser. As tasteless as a Rolling Rock no doubt. Perhaps there was no Guinness at the supermarket.

"I was out, ran into girl I know. I had met her way back, when I first came to America, and friend of hers. We went to Russian Vodka Room."

"But I called you all day!"

His eyes cloud over with that hooded and shifty look I instantly recognize from David.

"Oh no you didn't!"

The jealousy that the virgin couldn't inspire in me stabs me deep in the stomach.

He sucks on his beer, and shoots me a quick look.

"What?" His lips twitch.

Oh yes, I recognize that look, and the sheepish smile.

"Which one did you sleep with?" I keep my voice to a whisper. I don't want Ludivine to have any inkling of what transpires in the kitchen—thank God for inane, blaring TV commercials!

He glances at me, apparently weighing the pros and cons of honesty or deceit, balances on the fence for a brief instant, then opts for full disclosure.

"She's not even my type. I don't like blonds. I liked

her friend better, but I wasn't getting anywhere with her. I could see Milla was into me. She was giving me looks."

Milla!

"So you went to her place."

The sheepish look again, followed by a sip of Bud.

"She wanted to see how I balance on fist. So I brought up yoga mat. Then she gave me blow job."

"Shhhh. . . ." But the leap from yoga mat to blow job makes me laugh in spite of myself "Please. No details. I can imagine without your help."

Now we both burst into laughter. I stop laughing when I realize what should have been obvious.

"Wait. . . .You just came from there right now!"

For some reason, that stings more than knowing he's spent the night with Milla. Even though a few weeks ago, I was myself letting Bill kiss and grope me, I feel cheated on.

"I left you the keys to my apartment. I trusted you!"

"I didn't have to tell you. I decided to be honest with you." Hoooonest with the long "o".

True. He didn't have to tell me. I wonder what would have happened if David had been hoooonest. But how can a meaningless blunder like this be compared with what happened with my ex-husband? I bury the thought away. I hate the way it keeps festering, triggering in me the urge to hide it, instead of accepting how vulnerable I still feel.

"Mom, when's dinner ready?" Ludivine whines from the couch. "I'm hungry!"

To my utter amazement, the borscht is quite tasty. Rich and deep red, unctuous, laced with narrow slices of beef, razor-thin slivers of dill floating on the surface and a big wallop of sour cream. Even Ludivine asks for seconds and cleans up her plate. In spite of Yuri's judgmental frown, we are eating in front of the TV, the way we used to with David, at the end, when we were grateful for the sitcom dialogues to fill in the deadly silences. I have a real knack for creating dysfunctional families—no doubt from having been raised in one. They are reassuring in a way because so non-viable. It's the legitimate families that scare me, with their high-mindedness, and the horrifying possibility of remaining stable till the end, a suffocating jail from which one risks being stuck for life. As a child I always looked at my friends' "normal" families with a mix of envy and disdain. From the outside, they looked like impregnable fortresses.

Somehow, the Milla episode blows in the wind. After reading to Lulu and making sure she's asleep, I join Yuri in the guest bedroom, where he tumbles me silently, his hand on my mouth to smother any noise. At breakfast the next day, while he's still sleeping, Lulu complains about him in a low voice.

"He said American TV was stupid."

"Oh, he comes from another culture," I say, breezily. "You know what I think about the shows you watch. The same thing."

Offended, she looks up from her book. "But Mom, you like watching the Oscars."

I feel uncomfortable, hypocritical, caught in double-talk, but I figure everything is an occasion to teach.

"I know. You're right, I like the Oscars. Look, he is a little rough, but he didn't mean anything. It was just his opinion. He comes from another country, which used to be a communist country. America was their enemy."

"I hate him."

She looks at me with such fierce anger that I have to lean against the counter, seized with a new wave of vertigo.

## 3

The day before I leave for Vietnam, I meet my editor at a café on Irving Place. He's wearing ripped jeans and a flannel shirt over a white T-shirt, the kind of clothes David wore all the time, and that I loved to see on him, which causes my stomach to pinch. My editor must have taken the day off to read manuscripts.

"So, are you ready?"

"More or less."

I sit down across from him and he orders two café au lait.

"How's the book going?"

"Slow. You said I wouldn't be able to write well until I go there. I am making sure to make your prophecy come true."

He smiles. "I have something for you."

*The New Yorker* is open next to him on the table. I sip my café au lait. This is no time for nostalgia or regret. I am flying to Ho Chi Minh City tomorrow. My first trip to Asia! And when I come back, the words will fly out of my fingertips! From under *The New Yorker*, my editor retrieves a well-thumbed and dog-eared Lonely Planet guide to Vietnam, stuffed with stick-on page markers protruding like colorful little teeth.

"Take good care of it. It's a very special guide. It made our trip to Vietnam magical."

A faint odor of exotic flower and spicy food wafts from the pages of the guide when I open it. Maybe I'm only imagining the smells from the photos of fruit barges floating on the Mekong River and close-ups of frangipani flowers. My heart leaps in anticipation. Marguerite Duras. *The Lover*. Asia. Here I come!

\* \* \*

I have already read the labels on every bottle of eye makeup remover and face and eye cream at the duty-free shop, and tried on a half-dozen perfumes on my wrists to the point of nausea, and read every women's magazine horoscope in the newsstand, and visited the restrooms at least three times. Finally, at the gate, I cannot stand it any longer and I dial Yuri's number. Even though it's only eight PM, he sounds groggy.

"Ho Chi Minh City, where hell is that, why not Vladivostok?"

"It's the capital of Vietnam," I inform him. "Named after their famous communist leader, Ho Chi Minh. What's wrong?"

"I drank everything in apartment." Lugubrious voice, pitched low to elicit maximum guilt.

I swallow hard. I hear my plane being called. Singapore Airlines Flight 25 to Singapore with a stopover in Frankfurt.

"That's me," I say.

"What?"

"My plane. We're boarding. Why, what happened?"

He mumbles. "Depressed. Nothing going my way."

My seat number is being called. I get on the line and struggle with my bag and my cell phone, to get the boarding pass out of my purse.

"What do you mean?"

"I'm stuck here."

"What did you drink?" I've finally managed to get the boarding pass out. The attendant gives me a look, and slips it into the slot. The stub with the seat number pops out. She wishes me a good trip. I thank her and engage in the walkway.

"Sorry. I couldn't hear you. What?"

"Cognac, vodka, rest of wine."

Now it's obvious his voice is thick from hangover.

Furious, I hang up on him and hurry toward the plane. A second later my phone rings, his name shows up on the screen but I don't pick up. It is time for this to end, I think for the fifteenth time, as I drop into my window seat and unfold the blanket to wrap myself in to go to sleep. Maybe my trip will be a good opportunity to prepare for the breakup. "Vietnam is the key," my editor had said. Of course, he only meant the writing of the book.

It isn't. At least, not the way I imagined. Yes, the tropical heat, the smells of fruit and exotic flowers, the overripe stench of rotting fish, the balmy nights, the moon rising over the South China Sea, intoxicate me. I take copious notes on the landscape, the people, the smells, the colors, the colonial architecture. Scenes emerge which I quickly jot down. But something else happens too. Each day, as the driver I have hired takes me around the Mekong Delta, then up the coast toward North Vietnam, my life appears to me more clearly etched, vibrating with even more intensity, stripped of the usual clutter of daily details and problems that obscure the essential. Waves of tenderness for Lulu and for my mother swell my heart. And in the long night hours when I look for sleep, jetlagged by the twelve hours' time difference with New York, Yuri, like a wizard shape-shifter, appears to me draped in a luminescent mantle, and at other times under the mask of a demon. I struggle with his different incarnations, unable to tell which one is the real Yuri, thinking of Gogol's short story, "A Terrible Vengeance," in which a sorcerer bent on revenge keeps appearing to a young woman under various seductive guises to test her gullibility. By the time I fly to Hanoi, Yuri's incandescent, raw vitality has won out over his dark side, and he again threatens to dwarf my characters. I send postcards to Lulu and to my mother from Hanoi. In Hoi-An I buy a porcelain teapot for my mother's collection, a pair of cream, silk pajamas for Lulu, and a silk shirt for Yuri. And at the Singapore airport on the way back, I buy a cheap digital camera for me, and, on second thought, a bottle of Chanel Allure Homme perfume for Yuri.

# 4

New York. April. A cigarette stuck at the corner of his lips,
Yuri suspiciously sniffs the bottle of Allure Homme. When
he looks up I snap a picture of him with my new camera.
"No!" He covers his face with one hand as if I have just stolen
his soul. Too late. Now he tears through the tissue paper in
which the silk shirt is wrapped. I picked it in one of the tailors'
stalls at the Hoi An market, choosing a gray-green pattern
that I thought would bring out the color of his eyes, in the
largest size I could find, XXL. When I tried it on for size, the
cuffs were hanging a good ten inches past my fingertips.

I focus the camera on him again. "Put it on."

Cigarette still in his mouth, he slips on the shirt,
buttons it and struts in front of the mirror, moving his big
shoulders this way and that to assess the fit.

"Is that biggest shirt you could find?" A storm of fury
is gathering in his voice. It is true that the cuffs barely hit
his wrists and the shoulders look alarmingly tight. How
could I have possibly imagined that a Vietnamese XXL
would be a good fit for an XXL Viking seven feet tall and
unusually broad across the chest?

The more he moves, the more the silk strains until
it rips at the seams in a sinister tear. Satisfied, he looks at

me, his eyes defiant, and smashes his cigarette butt. It's obvious the whole scene is for show, to imprint on my mind the fact that I abandoned him and that my presents are woefully inadequate.

"You are such an asshole," I think, but afraid of his anger, I say nothing. I snap a picture of him in the ripped shirt, his shoulders bursting out of the frayed threads. I snap him when he claws at the glossy packaging of the Chanel Allure Homme perfume, extricating it out of its box, inspecting it from all angles. He sprays it under each ear, splashes it on like aftershave, and gives it two more vigorous sniffs. Then he picks up the airport plastic bag and tosses it dejectedly. "Oh, you just bought it at the duty-free shop."

I actually tested the Allure perfume and chose it for its oriental notes, which reminded me of the cheap aftershave he likes to douse himself with, but with more finesse. No point in telling him now. Certainly, it doesn't deserve this ugly rebuff.

I am so upset all I can manage is an angry, "give it back to me!"

But he ignores me and fingers the shirtsleeve like a tailor appraising a suspicious fabric. "Is silk?"

"Yes. I think so. Anyway, it doesn't matter whether it's silk or not. It doesn't fit you. Take it off."

He flings the shirt at my grandmother's old praying chair, on which I drape my clothes at night after undressing. Hopelessly damaged, it remains splayed over the velvet elbow rest, while he steps into the shower in the adjacent bathroom. I watch him lather himself. He grins at me with a gleam of cruelty, then splashes water on my feet.

"You have cellulite on your thighs."

So that's his revenge! How pathetic! I jump away from the water and shrug.

"So? Big deal."

I remember David, a few days before the end, leaning against the same shower wall, a towel tied around his hips, saying, "One day, there will be another man here in your life." Chances are it was a different kind of man he had in mind. Yuri leans forward and lifts my shirt.

"Come on, get it off."

He slides against the tiles and sits at the bottom of the shower, pulling me along with him. The soap on his cock burns me. His grin looks demonic in the shower steam. His back hits against the shower wall over and over. I close my eyes. His savage thrusts loosen all my pent-up anger. The angrier I am at him the harder I want to be penetrated.

"Shit!"

I open my eyes again. He peels himself off from the tiled wall and lets go of me. Through the cascade of water I see that the tiles are caving in behind his back. He pulls at one of them, which comes loose like a rotten tooth.

"Oh my God! What did you do?" I turn off the faucets and we both stand up. The tiles on the lower part of the wall are all coming loose. Yuri kneels by the loose tiles and pulls one after another repeating "Is garbage, garbage, garbage."

"No it's not. You banged too hard against the wall." Even to my ears, that sounds preposterous. But Yuri is so powerful it's easy to imagine that, like the big bad wolf who blows the little pig's house by huffing and puffing, he could make my shower wall collapse just by the sheer power of his back muscles. I drag him out, muttering that the repair is going to cost a thousand dollars at least, all my anger focused on the shower problem.

"You're only thinking about money."

"Money goes fast in New York."

With an angry flick of his wrist he tosses away the towel he has used to rub himself dry. I pick it up and hang it in a show of orderly domesticity.

"I fix shower," he says after a silence.

"You what?"

"I fix shower."

"You could do that?"

He shrugs, like, sure, but judging by his fits of temper and his unpredictability I have my doubts that he can apply himself to a task that requires craft and attention to detail.

An hour later, a knock at my door: a man I've never seen before, who, apparently, is rebuilding my downstairs neighbor's bathroom, is complaining that there's water dripping in the apartment. The man's biceps are entirely tattooed in a violent pattern of Japanese samurais and sabers. Yuri stares at them and promises to "fix shower." Yuri and I quickly go buy new tiles as well as a bucket of grout and appropriate tools. He strips down to his jeans and, half-naked and barefoot, sets to work. Meanwhile I head to my desk and try to immerse myself in Indochina. But every now and then I interrupt my scenes of opium smoking in the moonlight by the South China Sea to enter a demolition derby site where Yuri the giant is presiding over a chaos of broken tiles oozing grout. At the rate things are going it's obvious the work will take several days—which means several days of cohabitation with him. What about Lulu? What will she think when she comes back from school?

In spite of her previous fit of rage against Yuri, Lulu contents herself with a vague nod in his direction when he emerges from the bathroom, naked feet covered with dust, and she disappears into her bedroom while he pads over to the kitchen to pour himself a shot of vodka.

But when I tuck her in bed after dinner she whispers into my ear, "What's *he* doing here?"

"He's fixing the shower," I respond in the same whisper.

Her mouth and nose curve up in a grimace of distaste and doubt for his plumbing and tiling capabilities.

"He's sleeping here tonight?"

"Yes."

"Where is he sleeping?"

I keep my cool and tell myself that it's not really a lie.

"In the guestroom off my study."

"OK. *Bonne nuit.*"

Three days later, just as Yuri is finishing re-tiling, a knock at my door again. Grotesquely distorted, thick pale lips appear at the peephole. The man with the tattoos.

"The water's still dripping. Come and see for yourself."

How can it be? Yuri has fixed the tiles. Granted, they are crooked, the lines waving as if they had had one too many for the road, but still, thickly grouted. The biceps are waiting. The water is dripping. Steady. Drip, drip, drip. Chinese torture. "You've got to do something about this." The samurais' eyes bulge with hatred. Their open mouths show pointed sets of teeth under drooping mustaches.

My heart sinks. Vision of walls rotting away, ceilings collapsing, my responsibility engaged. Two Italian brothers, professional masons summoned in emergency, arrive the next morning to assess the damage and begin to rip up the shower floor. Apparently it wasn't built properly. Instead of the requisite zinc bedrock, a simple sheet of plastic was laid under the cement, and the water has infiltrated underneath. They have to rebuild the bottom of the shower. Now I see a whole row of dollar signs. At least, their explanations get Yuri off the hook. Yuri offers them vodka at the kitchen table. It's eight thirty AM and I see in their eyes that they're convinced they've come to the house of an alcoholic. They refuse a drink, but he pours himself a glass and volunteers his help. I watch him with disbelief. These two Italian masons are unlikely to let an amateur who starts his day with a shot of Stoli join their team.

# 5

Zibeyda calls me a couple of weeks after I've gotten back from Vietnam, and with her soft, lilting accent, invites us for dinner again. I bring along the manuscript, which I quickly finished reading. I can't wait to relieve myself of it. And sure enough, after an interminable parade of dishes, Zibeyda brings the tea tray to the low table in the living room, along with a bowl full of chocolates, and asks the question I was dreading.

"You read manuscript?"

"Yes."

"Did you like?"

"It's . . . very interesting."

Her face glows. Her pale hands stroke the couch on which we are both sitting. From the kitchen, where he is helping Babushka clear the table, Yuri says something in Russian that I don't understand and Zibeyda seems to argue with him. Still invisible, Yuri continues in English, "Tell her you want her to show it to publisher," before unleashing another round of Russian. Embarrassed, Zibeyda blushes.

"Don't pay attention to his moods," she whispers. "He's really very sweet guy, at heart. He has Russian temper. Husband like that too."

"I did read your pages. They are very lively. But you would need to work with an American editor."

Her eyes cloud over. Perhaps that's what made her a good actress, this ability to let her emotions emerge over her face, and then float away, seamlessly.

"I understand. You must be busy." And, before I have the time to say anything, she leans forward conspiratorially. "Of all women I have seen him with, you are best for him." Her voice lowers even more. "Do you love him?"

My heart leaps in terror. She lays her hand on mine. Her skin is so soft and pale it makes me think of an overripe pear, on the verge of decomposition. With a jerk, I pull my hand away.

"He needs woman like you."

"Maybe." I laugh uneasily. "But do I need a man like him?"

She smiles. Maybe she thinks I am joking. I smile too, but inside I shudder, as if a net has been spun around me. Both Yuri and Zibeyda are working me, pressing on my guilt, assuming that, by the sheer fact that I have more than they have, I ought to help them.

Yuri reappears in the living room in big gusts of words filled with guttural sounds and sliding vowels punctuated with great and repeated smacks of his open palm against the coffee table—a frightening outpouring of raw emotion. Babushka tries to calm him down, but nothing doing. I want to go home, but I've drunk too much vodka, I am tired, and it's dark. I don't have the energy to drive back to Manhattan, let alone New Jersey.

"You don't really care, do you," Yuri suddenly snaps at me.

"About what?"

Zibeyda makes a sign with her hand, meaning, don't pay attention to him.

Yuri's big hands come down on the coffee table again.

"You don't care about me," he says.

I have no idea what they have been fighting about, and why Yuri is suddenly turning against me at this moment, although his mood has been foul ever since I've come back from Vietnam, and even before. He paces up and down the living room with irrepressible energy. "You don't care about me." There's no point in defending myself. He is right. I don't care, at least not the way he wants me to care. The nuances would be useless to argue. I go sit on the other couch to get away from him, but he follows me and grabs my shoulder.

"Come. We're going home."

Home? I yank my arm away. "I am not going anywhere with you if you're like that."

Her fists on her hips, Babushka yells something at him in Russian.

"I am fine." He's making a tremendous effort to speak calmly.

I am scared. Not like when he had balanced me at the edge of the East River parapet. That was a game. But scared to be alone with him. I accept Zibeyda's offer to sleep on the couch.

When I wake up late the next morning, Yuri is calmly sitting on the other couch, where he must have slept. He brings me a cup of tea, cracking a stupid, unfunny joke.

No, I don't want to follow him back to his sad little apartment. The very idea of being his woman, with all that it implies, is revolting. The hunger I saw in Zibeyda's eyes, her hope that I could help her into my world echoes Yuri's own bitterness with me. I pack my bag in a hurry, while he watches me from the door with a grim face. When I pass him he grabs my wrist. Even without meaning to (and maybe he does mean to) his fingers feel like a vise grip.

He follows me outside. I fire up the engine of the Saab. He leans into the car window to kiss me goodbye. I turn my face away. His lips land on my cheeks. "Bye." I kick the gas pedal, eager to put the most distance between them and me.

# 6

May. Six thirty AM. The voice on the phone is French, with a slight southern lilt. A man I don't know. "It's about your mother."

I sit up in bed, my hands soaked with sweat. Woken up by the phone, Lulu pushes my door open, looking alarmed. My mother's just flown back to Provence from Helsinki. For the first time ever she felt too tired to drive to Finland, where she spends her winters. She is staying in her van in the village campground waiting for the people who are renting her apartment to leave in a couple of weeks.

"She's in the hospital," the voice goes on. "She had a cerebral hemorrhage."

"What? Who are you?"

"I am the one who called the *SAMU*. I think you'd better come."

Blank. It's the vertigo again, something spiraling, engulfing me.

"What's wrong, mummy?" Ludivine asks, stiff by the door.

"It's Nanny. She's sick. I have to go to France. You will stay with your dad. I'll come back in a few days I promise."

150

My uncle is waiting for me in the lobby of the hospital. I have driven straight from the airport, in a little rental Renault, holding my breath the whole way. I am dizzy with jetlag. In the waiting room of the ICU, we change into pale blue gowns, masks, gloves, and pale blue paper slippers over our shoes. When we walk into the room, I first see my mother's profile facing the window, like a flower leaning toward the light. The other side has collapsed—a landslide. Her mouth hangs, half-open. My heart splits apart.

"*C'ést moi maman.*"

A vague smile. At least she recognizes me. On her good side, her face still beautiful, her skin creased like exquisitely fine tissue paper. Her eyes unfocused. Looking her age, 85, for the first time ever.

"*Ça va bien maintenant.* I just had nausea. Now I'm fine." Her voice a thin fillet of sound I don't recognize.

Her bad hand lies dead on the white sheet. Her good one pulses into mine like a tiny bird. She had a heart attack thirteen years ago, and sailed through it. But not this time.

At the hotel restaurant where he has booked us rooms, my uncle tells me this story: he had gone to the garage one day to check if my mother's van was ready. "Ah, you're coming for the gypsy's van?" the garage owner asked. My uncle thinks it's funny. *La Gitane.* That's the name of the cigarettes in the blue pack, with the blue gypsy dancing away in smoke. My mother doesn't smoke Gitanes, but Benson & Hedges, or Craven A. The smoke of blond tobacco mixes with that of her tea and her perfume. I see her with one of the long cotton caftans she's been wearing lately. Like an African queen. Or a hippie. I've offered her one, in Indian cotton, a floral print in deep purples. The robe billows around her. She's always naked underneath in summer. "To feel freer." The gypsy sleeping in her van, carrying her bulging plastic bags. La Gitane. My uncle chuckles. I don't look at him. The old shame spreads like fire in my chest.

At the campground, the man who called the *SAMU*, the director of the camp, shows me to her van. A beached whale, stranded among the pine trees, the kayak rising on top of the roof like a prow, with its long, tapered ends. A garden table and two white plastic armchairs set up on a patch of grass. On the table an enamel basin full of water and a bowl with three peeled potatoes and a wood-handled pocketknife, the Opinel she never travels without. She was preparing lunch when it happened. Inside the van: the narrow bunk bed undone, used tissues crumpled on the front seat, a mess of tools and paint tubes, her clip-on sunglasses on the dashboard, a one-burner gas stove on the foldout table, a set of Chinese enamel dishes, chipped from use, Russian novels on the shelf, Andreï Makine and Vassily Grossman's *Life and Fate*, and one hardened, crooked baguette. I turn away, my stomach churning, as if I had just walked upon a crime scene.

# 7

The second cerebral hemorrhage happens four days later, on May 13, and this time my mother slips into a coma. David puts Lulu on a plane to Nice, and by the time I pick her up at the airport and drive the three hours back to the hospital, she's passed away. In the church during the funeral mass Lulu keeps pulling her hot, clammy hand out of mine and rubbing it against her skirt to pat it dry. My stomach lurches every now and then as if the pain were coming from the bottom of my stomach rather than from my heart, like when I ride in a car on a mountain road. Tears suddenly fill my eyes and dry out. The pain stays inside, deep in my guts.

The siren, the rebel who held the stage nonstop with her fits and curses, her dark moods that compelled me to take care of her as though she were my little girl, her spitfire eyes, her defiant, killer smile that made me want to wipe it off her face—that woman is gone. If I had loved her enough, would I have left her alone in New York, four months ago, after the new year, to fly to Paris with Lulu? If I had stayed with her would she still be alive? Lulu presses her sweaty hand into mine. There are only the two of us now.

My cell phone starts to chirp as soon as Lulu and I land at JFK on our way back from the funeral. A series of missed calls show up. I scroll down the screen. All from Yuri.

"What's the matter, *Maman*?" asks Lulu, who can read emotions on my face before I am even aware of them.

"Nothing." I turn off my cell phone, for fear he might call again, and hold her tight against me.

I only listen to his messages the next day, alone in the car. There are eighteen of them. Eighteen messages! Cold sweat runs down my back. I know your mother died. How can you not have called me from France? Where are you? Call me back. I need to talk to you, and so on. One message, clearly left in a state of inebriety, goes on for at least ten minutes.

\* \* \*

David has taken Lulu to the Hamptons. He will drive her directly to school on Monday. I've turned off my cell phone and am filtering my home calls. I bury myself in the Andreï Makine novel I found in my mother's van and brought back with me—*Tales of My Russian Summers*. Reading it is still communing with her, keeping her alive, but, in a twisted way, it connects me anew with Yuri. By Sunday evening, I can't stand it anymore, I pick up the receiver to call Yuri, change my mind before it rings, and hang up. I know I shouldn't call him, that the web that he and Zibeyda have thrown around my neck will only get tighter, but alone, without Lulu, the loss of my mother feels too heavy for me to carry. After the third, aborted attempt, I put the book down and dial his number for good. It's past midnight but he answers on the second ring.

He still sounds reproachful and angry, but his voice, just by being so alive, loosens the terrible burden that deadens me.

"Come now," he says.

The parkway is deserted. Even though it's dark, I don't mind driving tonight. Yuri is my refuge. My mother's cashmere scarf is wrapped around my neck. The one I gave her last Christmas. In a color she liked, oatmeal. The one she was wearing when I last saw her in New York. The last few years, she had been into white: white fur coat, white toque hat, white woolen sweater, pale leather snow boots. The scarf matched everything she wore. How her eyes had shone when she opened the wrapping, thrilled that I had gotten it right, or even that I had thought of her, always so grateful, so touched by any expression of love! Now it smells of campfire and the outdoors. It even has a few twigs still caught in the knit. She must have worn it on one of her long walks in the birch wood in Finland, and kept it on in front of the fireplace, in the log cabin.

Yuri is gaunt, like a man who hasn't slept or eaten in days, or who has lost his own mother a second time. Even more gaunt than after his breakup with Tasha. A heap of cigarette butts overflows on a saucer. Trays of amber jewelry are stacked helter-skelter on the kitchen table, tiny blown glass and amber animals spill out of a plastic bag, DVDs are scattered on the floor. A cooler is half-filled with bags of nuts, fruit, cartons of juice, as if he'd been trying to get ready for a fair, couldn't make it on time, and gave up at the last minute. His mood is foul.

"Why didn't you call me from there?"

155

"I couldn't," I lie. "I was busy the whole time with my family and Ludivine and I slept in the same room. I didn't have any privacy to call you."

"Pffft. . . . Is not good reason. I was going crazy here. I kept thinking of my mother. Didn't you get my messages?"

"Regular American cell phones don't work in Europe. I only got them when I came back."

"You could have called your voicemail. I couldn't sleep whole time you were gone."

I don't want to hear a barrage of reproaches. I don't want to have to explain anything and justify myself. I know I shouldn't have come, but I just need to feel his body against mine, his warmth. As a peace offering, I show him the scarf. He sniffs it. He likes that smell of outdoors.

We lay down together, still dressed, zipped into his sleeping bag, "my little casket," he calls it, his morbidity now appropriate. He pulls the scarf to him and wraps it around both of us. I tell him how my mother sometimes would carry her sleeping bag outside and sleep by the lake, while already in her eighties. How once she had lost her way in the woods up in Massachusetts in the wintertime, and she had spent the night jumping up and down to keep herself warm, and some hunters had picked her up and drove her back to her van. She was so thrilled to have made the headlines of the local paper that she kept the clipping in a folder.

"I would have liked your mother," he says.

The scarf has gotten warm between us. We are swathed in the woodsy cashmere as if in a cocoon.

"You're crying?" His tone turns rueful. "Your mother was eighty-five-years-old! Is normal she died. You are grown-up. What are you crying about, like kid!"

I sit up and pull the scarf to me. "It doesn't matter how old you are. It still feels like a terrible loss."

"Mother didn't get chance to grow old. When she died, she was younger than you now. Thirty-eight-years-old. Imagine that! Is unfair. You're still alive and she never made it to your age. You're acting like baby."

I jump out of the bed and start gathering my things. I was so wrong to come. What possessed me to think Yuri could share the loss with me?

His eyebrows arch in an ironic look.

"What are you doing?"

I don't answer.

"Is it because of what I said?"

"I'm going home."

"Home!" He snorts. "You're lucky to have home. I have no home."

When I come back from the bathroom with my toilet bag, he's up and standing at the front door, his arms stretched across the threshold to stop me, but he speaks softly.

"Don't leave. Please. Is almost dawn. Let's go to sleep. Tomorrow morning we take van and drive to beach.

Yuri parks the van on a parking lot by the shore, and strips to his Speedo. His tan shoulders and arms contrast with his pale legs and torso. A truck driver's tan. He spreads a blanket on the sand, kneels on it and pulls down his Speedo.

"Suck," he says.

I glance around us. Not a soul. The seagulls squeal far off, down by the edge of the water, which is at low tide. The sky is pure, except for the piercing white trace of a jet engine.

He holds out his sex to me like an offering, a fountain of oblivion. I fill my mouth with it, tongue slithering.

He gives me brief, monosyllabic orders: "Harder. Faster. Slow down. Swallow."

I wipe my mouth with the back of my hand and roll on my back next to him. My mind is entirely blank.

The sun is warm already. No wind. A perfect obliteration. He flips to his side and out of his daypack pulls out a small Poland Spring bottle filled which cranberry juice that must be laced with vodka. He takes a slug, screws the top back on and puts it away.

"I need your help," he says.

An icy frisson runs down my back, in spite of the sun. "What?

"I need you to marry me."

My heart starts to beat violently. I knew I would pay the price to have come to him. Even though the question of marriage has never come up between us, it was always there in filigree, like an invisible watermark on a dollar bill, that you only have to hold out to the light to see.

"What about that girl?"

"What girl?"

"The virgin."

"You don't care about me do you?"

I dig my fingers into the sand, make a funnel with my left hand and spill a little sand into it, all my emotions frozen.

"I thought you had plans to marry her."

"It's over."

"Why?"

"She met someone else. She got tired of me doing nothing. We had fight."

The sand escapes from the bottom of my hand with the slowness and inexorability it would have passing through an hourglass. "But Yuri, you know I am not a citizen."

He takes a long swig of vodka from the plastic bottle and screws the top back on.

"It works too, even with green card, I asked lawyer."

"Marry one of the Russian strippers—one of Tasha's friends. Most of them are US citizens."

Yuri looks indignant.

"Tasha's not stripper. She was trained as classical dancer."

"Whatever. Look. I have a daughter. If I were twenty-five and had nothing, I might do it to help you out. But I have too many responsibilities."

"I just heard there's going to be amnesty for illegal immigrants who are married with US citizens or residents. I have three months to file."

I scoop out sand more vigorously with both my hands. It scatters on the blanket and on his wrist. He wipes it off angrily.

Under the loose, warm sand, the earth is packed hard and cold. The image of my mother's white van rises before my eyes, the kayak perched on top and jutting out like a sentinel, the three peeled potatoes, the little cot. *La Gitane* with her billowing robes. I dig my fingernails deep into the earth.

"So, will you?"

I look at my fingers; my nails are black. I wonder if it's packed sand, or soil.

I shake my head. "I can't."

"You're selfish."

This time it's the wind that gives me shivers. It gets up with the tide, I've read that somewhere. Yuri's putting his jeans back on and his shirt. He takes a final hit of vodka and tosses the empty bottle toward the sea with a powerful shoulder movement. The bottle lands at the edge of the water, frightening a seagull away, and bobs up and down with the tide.

At the Japanese restaurant where we stop on the way back, the owner slaps Yuri on the back, American style, and takes us to a private booth.

"Is that where you take your other girlfriends?" I tease him, trying to diffuse the tension rising between us, the kind of tension that grips couples in serious disagreement. A gigantic tray of sashimi appears on the table. The waiter, after uncorking the Muscadet I have ordered, pouring some in my glass for me to taste, and serving both of us, carefully closes the curtain.

"Girlfriends!" Yuri snorts. "You're not girlfriend."

"I agree."

He looks at me pensively. "What are you then?"

"Does it have to be defined?"

He drinks his glass of wine in one gulp and puts it down.

"I don't know. I like it this way. But don't you see how screwed I am?"

"You could try to be sponsored by an employer." My

voice rings hollow. We both know better.

"Is bullshit. Doesn't work. Only way is to get married."

He skewers a spicy tuna roll with his chopsticks planted vertically and swallows it whole. His mouth half-full, his eyes piercing, he goes on: "You know that very well, that's how you got your papers here."

"Me?"

"Yes. You told me you got married for green card."

"No . . . I didn't mean it that crudely. It was kind of a joke. It was a real relationship. . . ." The moment I've said the words, I wish I could take them back. He leans forward, chopsticks pointing toward me.

"And we don't have relationship?"

"It's different," I say, avoiding his eyes.

What relationship is he talking about? What about the Brazilian girls and all the Catherine Zeta-Jones with their long, luscious black hair, waiting for him to ravage them? But on the other hand, we've been seeing each other for more than a year, minus his four-month marriage. I pick around the sashimi platter with the tip of my chopsticks. I have lost all appetite. He finishes the Muscadet, pulls the curtain aside to call the waiter, and asks for the bill. When it comes, he pushes it toward me and stares at me with a smug look.

"Your turn to pay this time."

I stare back at him for a second, really angry, but I let it slide. I toss my Visa into the tray. He watches me sign the slip with an insolent look in his eyes, pleased with himself.

161

# 1

Wrapped in my mother's scarf, lost in the smell of wood fire, lying flat on my back, motionless, unable to sleep, I'm trying to imagine what it's like to be dead, when the phone rings. Yuri.

"Have you thought about it?"

"About what?"

"The marriage."

I uncoil the scarf and sit up.

"But Yuri, I told you I only have a green card."

"It can work that way too. It just takes longer."

"It's not a good idea. You should forget about it."

"I don't have any other option. I only have three months until amnesty deadline. You're the only one who can help me."

When I finally fall asleep I dream that I am trapped in a windowless room. Two ropes tie the door handle to an invisible hook outside. One of the ropes is looped around the neck of a German shepherd that barks furiously when I try pushing the door open. I wake up with a start. A gust of cool air blows through the screen. I get up to close the window. A sulfurous glow infuses the sky, a refraction of all the lights left on in all the office buildings, all the apartments where someone doesn't sleep. The city that I once found so vibrant is pressing on me with all the weight of its yellow sky.

Every other week Yuri brings up the topic again. The deadline is approaching. Couldn't I help him? I, too, have gotten my green card by marriage, after all. It's as if I had to pay, sooner or later, for having gotten that coveted green card, so magically, through love. If I loved him wouldn't I spread the good fortune in my turn and marry him?

Love? Is that what this is about? How much I hate the word "love" used in that manner! First he had told me he couldn't love a woman other than his mother. Then he married Tasha "for love," and that didn't work out. He was finished with love. What we have isn't "love," is it? What we have isn't clear, to either of us. He had warned me not to get "addicted" to him. Then he had said that it wasn't a "sex affair." *Ya tebya lioubliou*, he might have mumbled one night, but did I even hear him right? I remember the night we stood under the tree in his backyard, holding each other tight like two teenagers. But like a prisoner in Plato's cave, what I felt wasn't love, only the shadow of love. Since David has left, my heart is locked. I cannot feel, I can only desire. Now Yuri is flinging the word "love" in order to get what he wants and I resent it. I reason with him. I encourage him to get back with the virgin and give her what she wants. She would make a good wife, he has said so himself. But his arguments are sharpened to a fine and poisonous point: I am selfish, I only see him for sex, I am using him. "What about you? What are you seeing me for?" It's not the same, he says. He is looking for a relationship, while obviously I am not. I don't need a man in my life. Only a man to fuck. Each barb lands with wicked accuracy. I hate the portrait of me that emerges from his comments: a free woman who is using a young stud for her own pleasure and won't give him anything in return. It strikes too close to home. At the beginning of *The School of Flesh*, the fashion designer paid the young bartender, like a man pays a hooker, to establish her power and assert that the relationship was purely mercantile. Later she compromised herself by inviting him to live with her and the power shifted to him. I had compromised myself with Yuri in the same way. "I should be gigolo," he mutters, pacing up and down his little kitchen while the kettle whistles, announcing another round of tea. "I go down to Miami Beach and get picked up by rich, old American woman. I heard there's lots of money to be made there." He looks at me with cold, gray eyes and hands me my mug. The image of him strolling past the art deco façades, at the arm of a jowly, bejeweled heiress is unnerving. Is this the way he sees himself? Only good enough to sell his sexual services? And is this the way he sees me? Not only older, but rich? My big apartment in Manhattan might have fooled him. Even though, for most of my friends, I am a struggling writer and divorced mother, I know that compared to him, I am living in cushy comfort.

He is relentless. When I get ready to drive back to the city, he rests his powerful forearms on the opening of the car window and leans in. "I am your part-time lover. You're always in and out, going back to your life." I make the left turn and wave at him. He stands ramrod straight at the edge of the road, his legs apart, looking forlorn, his hands in the pockets of his brand

167

new Abercrombie & Fitch cargo pants for which he has just bartered a sickle-and-hammer flag at his last crafts fair.

The phone rings. "She's had another hemorrhage," the voice says in French. She's in a coma. We don't think she'll make it." I pick up the phone, my blood pounding, before realizing it was a dream. The clock reads two AM.

"I am downstairs," Yuri says.

"What are you doing here?" I whisper, praying that Lulu hasn't woken up.

"I was in Brooklyn. Can I come up?"

I imagine him talking into his cell phone in his van, parked by the fire hydrant, like those guys you see in the neighborhood doing their shady business in the darkness of their car.

"No, you can't. You can't call in the middle of the night and expect me to let you come up."

"Uh-Uh!" As usual, he tries to laugh it off. "You want me to sleep in van?"

"I don't want you to do anything. Do what you want."

"You won't let me come up?"

"No." The more he insists the more I feel compelled to resist him.

"You're heartless, you know that?"

"Whatever."

"I'll sleep in van, then."

"I don't care."

I hang up in a cold sweat.

At nine AM the next morning the bell rings. He's waited for me to come back from dropping Lulu off at school. He knows my schedule.

"Can I come up now?"

"No. I'm coming down. I'll speak to you downstairs."

He's leaning against the side door of his van, dressed conservatively in a navy blue polo shirt, tan slacks, lace-up shoes. A magazine is rolled under his arm.

"I slept in van," he says.

"You don't look like it. Your clothes look well pressed."

"I changed."

"Where?"

"Doesn't matter."

I look over my shoulder, afraid to see one of my neighbors come out of the door. "Let's not stay here."

We walk down the block and sit on the stoop of another building. He gallantly sweeps one of the steps with his hand and spreads his jacket for me to sit on.

"Have you seen this?" He points to the cover of the magazine he's carrying. It's *Time*. He opens it to an article about immigration from the ex-Soviet Union. Thick lines in red magic marker are drawn around two paragraphs telling the story of an illegal immigrant from Lithuania who, after eight years in the States, has been deported back to Vilnius. He was working as a cook in a restaurant in the suburbs of Chicago and denounced by an anonymous tip. There's a picture of him in a DETROIT TIGERS T-shirt and a baseball cap. In spite of his all-American getup and the three-year-old daughter he has with his Mexican girlfriend—who herself has a green card—the INS officers threw him out. The article is a plea for the legalization of illegal immigrants who have integrated in US society.

I hand the magazine back to Yuri.

"You're not saying anything?"

"I agree." I try to keep my voice even to hide the surge of bad conscience that floods me. "Illegal immigrants should have the right to change their status without being deported."

"You're selfish. Don't you see that it can happen to me any day?"

"Nobody has denounced you."

Yuri gets up and paces up the sidewalk, hitting his thigh with the rolled-up magazine. When we arrive in front of my building he dramatically picks up my wrists in his hands.

"Marry me! I'll sign damned pre-something agreement."

A dark fear grips me, but not wanting to be seen arguing in the street, I invite him upstairs. From the smile that plays on his lips when we sit down at the kitchen table, I realize that he's scored a point.

"What?" I ask.

"Nothing."

"Don't try to make me believe that. There's something."

A sardonic gleam flashes in his eyes.

"You're not writing today?"

"I will, as soon as you leave." As if I could ever write after the argument we've had!

"But you're free until you have to pick up daughter at three?"

"I said I would start writing as soon as you leave."

"No. You're not going to write today." He flips a business card on the table. "You're coming to see lawyer with me. I'm afraid he's going to take advantage of me."

"What?"

He takes a sip of coffee and grins.

"Russian club in New Jersey sponsoring me. Strip club. All Russian chicks. They need Russian driver to drive them from Brooklyn." He smirks. "Since you don't want to marry me."

Forgetting that a few minutes before, he was begging me to marry him, I am so relieved to hear that he is pursuing other avenues to get his papers I don't mind going to the lawyer's with him. After all, I feel responsible for him. Even though his English is getting better, it's clear he wouldn't know his way around a law office. With his deficient sense of boundaries, he might yell at the lawyer, or storm out without anything being accomplished.

I put on a pair of lightweight, hound's-tooth black and white pants, a fitted black jacket and high-heeled pumps. He whistles when I come out of the bedroom. I can tell he's pleased to show up at the lawyer's with a stylish woman, who will give him credibility and help show him the ropes. He will show them that he knows how to handle himself in life—with women, at least. That he has what it takes.

We take a cab downtown. The office is on lower Broadway, conveniently located across from the INS. Almost everyone speaks Russian—the clerks, the clients, some of the attorneys. The whole place looks like a well-oiled machine set up to exploit desperate immigrants. How many generations of these lawyers' firms have existed since the beginning of immigration in America? Even though Yuri has an appointment, we wait for an hour before being admitted. Amazingly, he has prepared for the meeting. He pulls out a handwritten sheet of paper ripped from a spiral notebook, covered with tight annotations in Russian.

The lawyer is American. He gets impatient after the first five questions, which Yuri painstakingly translates. From the corner of my eye I see that there are at least thirty-five more on his paper. The questions are precise, but so convoluted and obscure, listening to them is like sinking into the mud of a confused mind. I try to rephrase them in more direct English. The lawyer focuses on me for a moment, then looks bored and reiterates what Yuri has to do to be sponsored by the owner of the New Jersey club. In particular, he has to prove that no American can do the job in his place. Yuri laughs. Is obvious. All girls Russian. He has to speak in Russian tongue to communicate with them. The lawyer doesn't laugh. It's not so obvious, a driver just has to know how to drive, any American with a driver's license can do that. Talking with the girls is beside the point. Yuri doesn't agree and starts arguing his point vehemently. The lawyer shrugs and takes out a stack of forms and explains how they should be filled, which ones are for the club owner, which ones for Yuri.

After glancing at me again, pointedly this time, his eyes swivel back to Yuri.

"Is that your girlfriend?"

"Yes," Yuri says.

Oh! Now I am his girlfriend?

"Huh…," I start. What am I going to say? Not really? I am just a friend? A vague acquaintance? We just met downstairs in the street and he asked me to come up with him?

172

"You know," the lawyer interrupts me, his eyes now on Yuri. "The best way to get your papers is to get married. In six months you have your work permit. In a year you can leave the country, come and go as you please."

Yuri glares at me. Are the two of them in cahoots? Or has the lawyer come up with the idea all by himself, on the spur of the moment?

Yuri slips the forms into his briefcase and we take the elevator down.

"Did you hear what the lawyer said?"

"About what?"

"Marriage."

"Yes, I did."

"So?"

"I don't know. I'll think about it."

The boyish grin appears, revealing, rather endearingly, his chipped tooth.

"So you might say yes?"

All I have to do is to say no. But I can't. Is it because, in spite of not wanting to be Yuri's girlfriend I don't want to lose him? Because I am "addicted" to him? Because the fear of loneliness is even greater than the hazard of ill-advised entanglements? Because I am the privileged one, the one who has her life together—well, sort of together—a home, a child, enough money to live comfortably, and if I don't extend a hand to someone who's alone, on the outs, who needs my help, then I can't live with myself at all?

"I have to go home. And then pick up my daughter."

He studies my face, trying to figure out if I am being elusive again. Sadness spreads over his features.

"You don't love me."

He fires up a cigarette and leans against the window of a Domino's. Compressed in the pair of slacks and the polo shirt, briefcase in hand like the businessman he's dreamt of becoming, he looks defeated. How humiliating it must be for him to need me to get his papers. And yet I can't help feeling that I am just fair game for him, a Western woman he can push around, whose bad conscience he can play on to get what he wants.

Two days later, he calls me, sounding upbeat. Club owner has agreed to sponsor him, but he needs help. Can he stop by, he'd rather explain face-to-face. I agree to meet him for lunch at the same diner where he had first given me the bottles of wine.

"OK," he says, after attacking his omelet. "Owner needs $3,000 to pay for expenses. Filing, paperwork, lawyer's fee, all that. I don't have money right now. I'm still paying off credit card debt. Can you loan me? I pay all of it back, I promise."

Three thousand dollars. The shower, as I had foreseen, cost me $1,000. But I still have enough to last me through the end of the year, and by that time, no doubt, I will have handed in the second part of my manuscript and gotten another chunk of my advance on royalties.

"I promise. I can pay you back by end of summer. With interest," he adds, ever the businessman.

Three thousand dollars. The sum is large, but not so large that it would be a problem if I never got it back. On the other hand, it's large enough to appease my sense of responsibility. I watch him devour the rest of his omelet and clean the plate with bread, while the knot in my stomach loosens up. Blackmail victims must experience a similar, short-lived respite at paying off their tormentors.

"So?"

We walk together to my bank, at the corner of Broadway and 8th Street. I withdraw the three thousand in cash and hand him the bills. He writes a receipt, pledging to reimburse me by September 1 "with interest." What is three thousand dollars, after all? It seems a small price to pay to buy my freedom.

## 2

July. Lulu and I fly back to Nice for the family wedding we were going to attend with my mother. It's a bittersweet trip; the warmth of a family reunion with my cousins and their children cheers me up but at the same time stirs painful memories. When I go to bed at night, after dancing under the stars of Provence, I stay awake for a long time, jet-lagged, longing for Yuri, as if he were the only person who could fill my mother's absence.

I call him as soon as I get back in New York, excited to see him again, but his sharp voice makes me tense up, fearing that his bad mood is caused by an immigration problem. But no. He is upset because he has to leave for Marin County in a few days and he's not ready. At the last minute a friend has asked him to do a series of crafts fairs in California and he has "million things to do" before he goes.

"How long are you staying in California?"

"A month."

I feel a twinge of regret that we'll hardly have any time together before he leaves.

"I'll drive you to the airport, if you want. I could come on Saturday and take you to Newark on Sunday."

"OK. Is good. I want to see you before I go."

But when I arrive on Saturday, he still hasn't snapped out of his dark mood. He watches me in gloomy silence while I put the groceries I've brought with me in the fridge, and suddenly grabs my waist. He runs his hands down my stomach and pushes them crudely between my legs.

"You came to provoke me. You travel all the time and I'm stuck in the States. I can't even go to Moscow to visit my mother's grave."

I am dumbstruck by his words. I resent Yuri's use of his mother's death to make me feel guilty every time I take a trip, especially since I have come to help him. He looks at me with that insolent look, undressing me with his eyes. Then he removes a half-full liter of vodka from the freezer. He pours himself a shot and drinks it bottoms up.

"Want some?"

I shake my head.

"Why you wore that dress?"

"What do you mean?"

"Revealing like that?" He points at my bare back and shoulders. "Did you wear it in France?"

I look at him square in the eyes, challenging him.

"So what?"

Another shot of vodka. He rummages around the fridge, extracts the cheddar I've brought, and slices it on a plate. He swallows a piece then pushes the plate toward me. Another shot. Hyper aware of my naked shoulders, of my breasts loose without a bra under the flimsy cotton fabric, just tied behind my neck, of my naked feet with the coral-colored polish, I watch the level of vodka go down.

"You are doing that on purpose, to turn me on."

"Doing what?"

"Don't pretend you don't know what I mean."

"So?"

I am playing with fire. His slow-burning embers are doused with alcohol, ready to ignite.

"Don't look at me like that," he says.

"Like what?"

"Press the button on the stereo," he orders me.

The stereo is standing on the counter, at my elbow, its cord coiling around the stove and plugged into the wall on the other side. I extend my arm toward it and press the ON button. The Patricia Kaas cassette he made me listen to once on the phone explodes in the room. I am about to turn down the volume when he fires another order.

"Don't. Leave it like that."

The music pulses, the singer's sultry voice fills up the small room, loud like the sound track of a thriller.

Another shot of vodka.

I stare at the bottle. Almost empty.

The bass pulses like a heartbeat.

Another shot. That's it, the bottle is empty, he upends it over his glass and tosses it toward the trash can, his shoulder muscles bulge and contract, good throw, the bottle describes a neat arc, neck first, shooting down, oops! It misses the trashcan by half an inch, smashes against the wall right by the stereo plug. Crrrrk! A rain of glass at the foot of the counter, huge chunks bounce on the linoleum, vibrate a second, come to a rest. I stare at the glass, and at my naked feet. I don't move.

Bottoms up again. He's got his hand around the glass, tight, his knuckles white. I wait for the sound of broken glass again, for the sight of blood running between his fingers. He looks at his hand, then gently lets go of the glass. He gets up heavily, he only has three steps to be on me. I don't move. There's glass everywhere around us. He carefully avoids the shards and runs his hand up my naked legs, underneath the dress, up the crotch.

"No underwear. Bitch!"

He pulls his hand out and sucks his fingers with a grimace.

"You like to see me go crazy don't you?"

My heart is beating violently. He picks me up by the waist, just as he had that far away day in the East River Park, and plunks me on the counter. Pulls my dress up and spreads my legs open, pushes his face inside of me.

The boom box is right next to me. I feel the bass against my arm. I lean back on my elbows. He devours me with his mouth. I feel myself coming, I can't help it. I scream.

He unbuttons his jeans and enters me. The stereo is still pulsing against me, Patricia Kass in a loop. Then he carries me to the bed, still screwed tight inside of me, my legs around his waist, careful to avoid the broken glass. He rides me hard until I come again, and again.

"Whore," he says into my ear, "you like it when I am wild. You want it again, don't you? How many times did you come?"

It's his rage that fires me up. His unbridled energy releases a dangerous hunger in me. The violence is what I want, something dark and smothered in me has been woken up. I can't stop coming. I scream so loud he gags me with his hand. I bite it hard.

179

"What the f . . . ?"

He shakes his hand up and down and laughs. From where I look at him, below, his face is distorted like that of a demon carved on the peristyle of a Gothic church. He rolls off me and pushes me hard away from him, until no part of my skin touches his. I curl into a ball and pull the sheets over me.

During the night I smell his Parliaments. In the dim light, wreathes of smoke float like a fog. He is sitting at the kitchen table. From the bed I can't see what he's doing. I only glimpse his back and the back of the chair. The glass clinks.

"I hear there are jobs in Alaska," he's saying. "Fucking get away from everything. I'm able body. That's what they're looking for. They don't care about brains. Just able bodies. Strong muscles. Like horse. Strong like horse. I'm talking to you. Do you hear me?"

"I'm trying to sleep."

"I'm fucking trapped, here. I can't even go see mother in Moscow."

"Your mother's dead."

"Every year I put flowers on mother's grave. In wintertime. White lilies on white snow. Just like when she died. The snow all over her coat."

He chain smokes. The smoke is getting thicker, bluish in the rays of light.

"Come to bed."

"Don't tell me to go to bed. You have no fucking right to tell me anything." He pulls back his chair, and I see him now, leaning forward, elbows on his knees, face down, his biceps bulging out of his white tank top like Marlon

Brando in *A Streetcar Named Desire*. I don't know which part I am playing, Stella or Blanche. When I wake up again much later, a gloomy light seeps around the window and he is bringing me a cup of coffee in bed.

"Sorry about last night." He sounds calm and genuinely apologetic.

I sit up and drink from the cup. It's Turkish coffee, fragrant and strong.

"Are you ready for your trip?"

He gathers his dirty laundry in a bag and the bottle of detergent and carries them to the kitchen.

"No. I have to do laundry. We go later. I'm hungry."

He pulls the frozen caviar out of the freezer, carves a small piece and feeds it to me from the tip of the knife. The caviar is so cold it's tasteless. Then he takes another bottle of vodka out—a smaller one than the one he finished the night before, and pours himself a shot.

"Forget about your laundry. We'll never make it on time to the airport."

Instead of answering, he drinks another shot and pushes the tin of caviar toward me. "Eat."

"I'm not hungry."

"Come here."

He picks me up from my chair and sits me on his lap. I feel his erection under my dress.

"Stop it. What about your flight? You should be packing." I slither off his legs, pick my way carefully through the broken glass and go to his bedroom to put my shoes on. Then I watch him get drunk from the door.

"You come, you go. Whenever you feel like it. What about me? You don't even care, do you?"

"I cared enough to come all the way here to drive you to Newark. But if you don't pack, you're going to miss your flight. If you don't stop drinking and get ready now I'm out of here."

"Where are you going?"

"Home."

The big jar of laundry detergent is at his feet. He picks it up and tosses it toward the bedroom door, right by me. I barely have the time to dodge behind the wall before the bottle explodes and the detergent spills in a sticky mess all over the linoleum.

"Are you crazy?"

My blood is pounding. The oozing blue liquid, the broken glass from last night, the bottle of Tide ripped open, the stereo still blaring the same sultry pop songs. This squalor can't be my life.

"I didn't even see you." With an ugly scowl he stares at the flow of blue detergent in which swims the broken glass. "Go get mop and clean up mess."

"You're insane. You made it. You clean it. I'm leaving."

"No, you're not. Go get mop and go down on your knees."

I want to laugh at his ludicrous order, but I'm terrified. His voice is threatening. Anyway, it's impossible to even cross the kitchen without slipping in the blue liquid and falling into the glass shards.

"Here." He picks up an old cloth drying on the windowsill and tosses it at me.

"On your knees!"

I squat and wipe around. I'm totally ineffectual. But I manage to absorb enough slippery blue liquid to clear a less dangerous path to the door.

He points his foot, dripping with detergent, toward me. "Now wipe feet."

"What? No way!"

His shoulders slumped, he stares at the mess for a while, then makes his way across it, passes me at the bedroom door, and lies down on the bed. I watch him for a moment to make sure he's asleep and tiptoe outside through the narrow path I've cleared, toss my bag into my car and turn on the ignition. My cell phone rings just as I am getting onto the Garden State. I don't pick it up. Flashes of his white Lincoln tearing after me to set up siege in front of my door keep me pressing way past the speed limit.

Instead of heading East across town, I swing up the West Side Highway and make a right toward 23rd Street and from there take Lexington to Gramercy Park. I find a spot at a meter and check into the Gramercy Park Hotel. The old Gramercy Park Hotel, before it was renovated and gentrified. I drop my bag and call David and ask him to keep Lulu for the night. I tell him I'm upstate and my car broke down. Nothing serious, something wrong with the carburetor. It'll be fixed in the morning. Then I call Yuri, get his voicemail, and leave him a message to tell him it's over, that I never want to see him again nor hear from him. From my window the streetlights make the trees and bushes of Gramercy Park look like London, elegant and safe, light-years away from Yuri's world. I've just landed in the city, and this night is the beginning of a new life.

I go to sleep without eating.

At home I unplug my landline. Yuri's name shows up seven times on my cell phone. At three PM I pick up

183

Lulu at school. In the evening we order Indian curry, her favorite food, and after dinner we huddle together on the couch, wrapped in each other's arms, in front of the TV, soothed by a show on Nickelodeon. I still have a banging headache like after a massive hangover, but the giddy relief of having survived a narrow escape is exhilarating.

* * *

"Yuri not well," Zibeyda is saying on the phone. It's been three days since my escape. My throat tightens as soon as I hear her soft accent, her gently rolling r's. I have answered by mistake, I was only screening the calls from New Jersey. Her number had an innocent 718 prefix.

"He's in California, working with Ruslav. He's very upset. He has bad temper, I know. But is good guy. What happened? He had been drinking?"

"I don't want to talk about it."

"His mental state not very good."

"He asked you to call me?"

"No, no . . . I wanted to know what happened. . . ."

"Tell him I wish him good luck. But it's better if I don't ever see him again."

After I hang up, I triple lock my door and look outside the front windows, afraid to see his white Lincoln or his gray Dodge van magically parked at the fire hydrant.

# 3

August. The sun sneaking through the Venetian blinds
of my study carves narrow stripes of light and shade.
Under the *woosh* and *swoosh* of my ceiling fan stirring a
hot breeze on my forehead, I scribble page after page. In
the sultry New York heat, I imagine Mimi, my *café-concert
chanteuse*, lying in the Governor's arms, drenched in
sweat. In Saigon, the blades would be made of wood, but
they wouldn't smother the stench of rot arising from the
gutters just outside. Lulu is at the beach with her dad for
the whole month, until Labor Day. The big apartment feels
empty without her laughs. And even though my mother
and I had a difficult relationship, the memories of our tense
moments have vanished, leaving behind only the terrible
sense of loss. I miss our days in Provence, our dinners on
the terrace, the spicy smell of her Benson & Hedges, the
taste of our *panachés* in the cafés, her ferocious vitality, the
deafening racket of the cicadas, our summers so brutally
cut short. But at least, relieved of Yuri's oppressive
presence, I can finally write steadily and make progress.

The orange Post-it on which I once wrote his phone
number is still pasted on my bedside table. I used it as
bookmark for the Modiano novel I started after breaking

up with him. And then for all the other Modiano novels I have been reading, back to back, one after another, every night, before going to sleep.

At the beginning of the month my old friend Stéphane visited me from Paris with his new girlfriend, Sofia, a Hungarian video artist I immediately got on with. We had long brunches in the kitchen, took walks in Brooklyn and in Central Park, cooked dinner together and carried our trays upstairs to the roof to enjoy a little coolness and the spectacular Manhattan skyline. But their presence made me nostalgic for my life with David, for the kind of relationship I feared I might never have again. The day they were to fly back, we sat down at the kitchen table for breakfast, the sun splashing among the bowls of *café au lait*, and the conversation turned to Budapest and Moscow. I told them about Yuri and the violent scene that led to the end of our affair.

"Russians are crazy," Stéphane said. "Be careful."

Before going back to France for my mother's last days, I had taken a picture of Yuri leaning against the kitchen counter, a cigarette at his lips, near where the three of us were sitting. He hated that picture. Because he had decided many times to stop smoking, he didn't want to be seen indulging in that "crap." But he had insisted that I show it to my mother in the hospital. "Tell her I send her best wishes." I was touched by his offer, and I would have showed the picture to my mother if she hadn't been so ill.

"He has a Russian temper," I protested. "But he's a good guy." The very words, I realized afterwards, that Zibeyda had used. Sofia didn't say anything, but she looked doubtful.

The heat is more and more crushing. Because we usually spend our summers in France, even when I lived with David, we never installed A/C. I plug two fans on either side of the bed, each one blowing straight into my face. But I still need to get up in the middle of the night to take a cold shower, and lie down, dripping wet, on a towel, to cool out for a few minutes, only to start again a couple of hours later. One night, in the tropical heat, like a sleepwalker or a junkie who's recently gotten clean and deludes herself that she can safely snort a pinch of the powder or shoot up just one time, I peel off the Post-it and call Yuri in Marin County.

"Why you let me down?" His first words. His voice incoherent. Bitter. Reproachful. Not even hiding the satisfaction of having won, since I am the one who called. Immediately, like the time I had phoned him from the Cherry Hill school, I regret my impulse. Too late. To ease out of the conversation as quickly as possible I try to it pass off as friendly. But, like any pusher, he knows he's got me. He calls me back a week later. His voice is upbeat, serene. He has stopped drinking and smoking, he tells me proudly. He is calm, stable. Stable—the exact word my mother used when talking about her mental state in Finland. "I am calm, stable there." An alarming word, because it can so easily flip to its opposite. "California very good for business," Yuri continues, "very good for health." And, by the way, would I pick him up at the airport?

He bursts out of the revolving door, pushing a cart loaded with luggage, his skin a handsome caramel tan, bursting with his old energy. He leans into my car window and hands me an envelope. I open it while he fills up the trunk. There are thirteen $100 bills in it and a note promising the remaining $1,700 ASAP. I am impressed by his punctuality and his *hooonesty,* and I cheerfully drive him back to his place, convincing myself that I am only giving him a ride, and that I will turn around and head back home as soon as I have dropped him off. But by the time we pull into his driveway, my good intentions fly out the window. I've come all the way out there, why not stay the night and drive back the next day? And when, at breakfast the next day, he invites me to join him at the Maryland State Fair the following weekend, the idea of escaping New York's unbearable heat for a rural getaway sounds downright terrific, the very thing I need to cool out and ease my grief.

* * *

From a distance, I catch a glimpse of Yuri at his stand, clipping a necklace around the neck of a heavyset woman with bleached, feathered hair. He positions a hand mirror in front of her so that she can admire how the pendant hangs down the opening of her tank top which threatens to rip under the pressure of her gigantic breasts. Next to them, the hand mirror looks absurdly dainty in Yuri's hands. Lightheaded, I lean against a stand down the aisle. What am I doing here? Just as I am weakly considering turning on my heels and driving straight back, he notices me and waves at me with a big smile.

I have taken my laptop with me and I spend my first morning writing in the motel room cluttered with Yuri's clothes and merchandise, then drive to the fair at lunchtime to "help out." Yuri likes the idea that we are working together as a team, and he keeps me busy—and away from my computer—by giving me little chores to do, like getting him coffee, reorganizing the tables and cleaning the glass display cases. When he steps away for a smoke, I wait stiffly like a sentry, wishing I were in my mother's place in Provence instead of having rented it for the summer and put it up for sale.

In the afternoon Yuri plays Russian folk music on his new tape player and announces "special late afternoon sales" with a booming voice. His nesting dolls fly off the shelf, especially his line of dolls with the likeness of Putin and Clinton, even though the Clinton years are long over. Just as we are beginning to close, a skinhead hovers by. After a short, whispered exchange, Yuri lifts the Soviet flag in front of which are displayed his collections of KGB and NKVD insignia and his pirated DVDs of the latest Hollywood blockbusters, and takes him behind. A few moments later, the skinhead slinks away, a poster rolled under his arm. Yuri waves to me with a mysterious air and lifts the Soviet flag again to show me what he's hiding: a secret stash of neo-Nazi posters.

The sight of the lighting-shaped, double SS of the Luftwaffe and the swastikas makes such a display of anti-Semitism, that I feel sick in my stomach and I walk away, but Yuri runs after me through the crowd, grabs my arm and spins me around. I stare into his pale eyes, which seem even paler with his tan, and, for a split second, I glimpse the metallic gaze of an enraged, alienated man.

"Don't take it so seriously," he coaxes me, his familiar irony snapping back. "I don't believe in that shit. Someone gave them to me to sell. Let's close stand and

189

get out of here. I want to go bungee jumping. First time."

Floodlights illuminate the bungee jumping net like a theater set. The air is warm, saturated with the greasy smells of barbecue and fries. The attendants strap Yuri into the leather apparatus. His body slowly gets lifted in the air, balances for a moment like a huge doll, then tips over, diving down in a heart-stopping moment before rebounding on the net. "Is fear that's exciting," he announces when he lands, his eyes shining with a fierce glow, and straight away asks to be sent up again, as if each jump were a hit of crack cocaine he craved again as soon as he had landed. "Wanna try?"

"I have vertigo, remember?" I sit down on a bench and watch him jump over and over, late into the night, with the same fixed revulsion I had watched him get drunk that night before the summer. "Is fear that's exciting." Even in my deluded state of mind, I cannot fail to see that Yuri and I share the same twisted fascination with fear.

Still fueled with adrenaline, he erupts into a furious harangue before we even get to the motel. He "hasn't heard from lawyer about sponsoring application, and deadline passed today." So it was all waste of money. If only I hadn't been so selfish! America let him down and I let him down. Now he has to go back to his initial plan: *get married*. I freeze at the sound of those two words, get married—which I naively thought had long been buried—as if he were once again pumping his fists at my door to shake me down. I slip into bed, my back to him. He immediately falls into a deep sleep, but I toss and turn, his words hanging for a long time in my mind. I know I should stop seeing him for good this time, but no sooner has the idea formed in my mind, than a thick fog descends over me, paralyzing all thoughts of action.

The day of my birthday, Yuri calls me from Manhattan, he has a present and a surprise for me. Can he stop by? Just a quick visit. He has "business meetings" in the afternoon. He hands me a red rose wrapped in cellophane and a present: an Internet method for learning Russian, with an interactive CD to download to my computer. He keeps the surprise for last: 90 twenty dollar bills that he spreads one by one on my bed, covering it all in a sea of green, and a piece of paper torn off a motel memo pad on which he has written FINAL PAYMENT $1800 *SPACIBO*!

He's beaming, proud to be making the deadline. "I said summer, remember?"

"That's too much! You only owe me $1,700."

"That's for miscellaneous and interest."

I peel off five twenties and press them into his hand. "Thanks, Yuri, but you don't have to do that. I'm not a bank."

His face turns white. "I told you from start I was *hoooonest*, that I pay you interest." His voice is tight, his whole body has turned rigid. "You don't decide how much I give you back. Buy yourself other present for your birthday."

The next day, instead of writing, I load the CD, and the Cyrillic characters crowd my computer screen while the voices of "Svetlana" and "Boris" fill my study with their soft, sensual Slavic accent. I close my eyes and, prompted by the voices, I repeat the long, complicated words in a low voice. When I first arrived in the States, I wrote down the new English words I learned each day in a little notebook, with their French translation. I would cover the French with my hand and I would repeat each word until I got it right, absorbing the culture along with the sounds of American English. Now the voices of Svetlana and Boris carry me all the way to the train tracks outside Moscow where a young woman lies, wrapped in a black coat, under a blanket of snow.

# 4

September. The weather is still gorgeous in Manhattan a week after Labor Day. On Tuesday, like every morning, I drive Ludivine to school; on my way back I turn on Z-100, but instead of the disk jockeys' usual banter, a grave voice announces that a plane has crashed into the World Trade Center. On impulse, I turn around to pick Lulu up. By the time I reach her school, the Pentagon has been hit. We go home and huddle together in front of the TV, cut off from the rest of the world without phone or email, watching the towers crumple down in clouds of smoke, over and over, the same images, like a giant video game on rewind. The next day, we venture outside and walk the deserted streets of the East Village poisoned with an acrid stench. From a distance, down the empty expanse of Second Avenue, the plume of black smoke mushrooming into the pure blue sky looks like those pictures of the bomb exploding over Hiroshima.

"Is it war, Mom?" Lulu asks me, her hand pressed into mine.

"No. Well . . . it's a kind of war. But war is much worse than this." I tell her about the trenches of Verdun, the German occupation of Paris, the bombing of London, the blitzkrieg, the concentration camps, the 20 million Russians massacred in WWII to push back Hitler, as Yuri never fails to remind me. We go to sleep together in my bed, our arms wrapped around each other. When the phone line is restored, the calls pour in from the rest of America and Europe. Yuri is the first one to call. He sounds upbeat, ironic, as if he had booked a ringside seat at the world's biggest fight and was enjoying the entertainment. "Take pictures of smoke," he orders excitedly. When I tell him how nervous we are, waiting for the other shoe to drop, he laughs at my "paranoia" and invites me over for the following weekend "to relax in country." At the sound of his warm, easy laugh I picture his backyard with its patch of green grass, the picnic table of weathered wood, the sparrows and the mugs of tea we drink outside on warm days—which has now become, by a stunning reversal, an oasis of peace and normalcy.

On Friday night, after dropping Lulu off at David and his girlfriend's beach house, I drive straight to Yuri's. He's waiting for me at the door of his "country house," a cigarette at his lips. I flick my fingers at it.

"I thought you'd quit?"

"It's crap, I know." But he swears he hasn't touched liquor in two months. Foolishly, I put great stock in his determination and self-control. His diligence in paying back his loan and his discipline staying on the wagon impress me. Perhaps he can reform? I am so relieved to be far from Manhattan, I immediately lie down and sleep for twelve hours straight, my anxiety vanished, as if I had traveled a long distance during the night and landed on another, safer planet. In Yuri's world there's no fear of terrorist attacks, only an ironic detachment about America.

The sound of the TV wakes me up. CNN is showing photos of the terrorists. They have the air of cartoon villains with their sinister looks and inky beards. Especially the suspected leader, Mohammed Atta. Raven hair, low forehead, fiery, coal-black eyes. Even blacker, more sinister than the others.

"Look at his eyes." Cross-legged on the bed, Yuri points the clicker toward the screen as if he could freeze-frame it. In fact the image remains frozen for a long second for the viewers to soak it up. Under the bushy brows, the eyes stare into the void. The eyes of a fanatic. "He didn't back down." Yuri's voice shakes with awe. "Imagine what it must have been like, just before he crashed tower. Going straight into death. He had balls."

Horrified, I try to wrestle the clicker out of his hands. "Stop it. Turn this off."

But he shoves me aside and presses the clicker again and again. The coal-black eyes appear on every channel. He turns toward me, his face transfixed.

"Did you see his eyes? I wish I had been in his place. Die for a cause and show Americans what it is to be man."

His pale eyes are burning with the same fanaticism and hatred, as if his own crushed pride and frustration with America had finally found glorious redemption: becoming a kamikaze.

"You're sick." The realization that Yuri has turned a corner into serious craziness hits me with crystalline clarity. My heart furiously beating, I swing my legs off the bed to get up and away from him.

"Where you going?" He stops me with a powerful

grip on my wrist. He clicks off the TV and pulls me back, his eyes now pleading. "Please don't go. I'm sorry. I didn't mean it. Stay with me."

He makes a pot of tea while I get dressed, and brings the two mugs to the picnic table in the backyard, which looks just the way I had imagined before coming, the sparrows hopping about and the inviting little bench. I sit down and he wraps his arms around my shoulders.

"Cheer up, stop taking everything so seriously. You know I have temper. I lose it sometimes. Means nothing."

I place my hands on his without saying anything. In the brilliant September sun, the visceral fear Yuri's fanatic words have aroused in me fades. I lean back against his chest. As frightening as his violent moods can be, his powerful presence is oddly soothing, reassuring, like an oak that plunges its roots way deep into the ground. It's that "Russian temper" Zibeyda talked about, a temper that fires him up, takes him to the edge of insanity and cools out just as fast as it has flared.

"Is just frustration. I love America, but America doesn't love me back." He laughs at his own joke.

* * *

The matrimonial lawyer has been recommended by a friend. She gives me an appointment a couple of weeks later, at her home, a sunny apartment near Lincoln Center. In a relaxed, intimate conversation, she tells me she has once been involved with a man not unlike Yuri. She even married him. And later divorced him. She explains in detail how a prenup agreement works. Although it's

196

never entirely airtight, "It's doable," she says. "You can protect yourself, and then divorce him when his papers come through."

I walk all the way home after the meeting. The streets smell acrid from the smoke at Ground Zero. Manhattan is still a ghost town—in spite of the cars which have been allowed back—the walls covered with photos of the WTC victims. Candles are burning, surrounded with sprays of dahlias and mums. I see Yuri's face at every street corner, his shoulders slumped in his wife-beater, desperate. A victim, an illegal immigrant whose only chance to work and establish himself in the States, given the law of this country, would be to marry a US citizen. *If you loved me wouldn't you marry me?* So many of my European friends have gotten their green cards that way. A quick stop at City Hall, a handful of "wedding pictures," interviews at the INS office. I know the drill by heart. A wait of a year, maybe two now—after what happened the government is going to get more and more suspicious. And voilà! He gets his papers and we divorce, amicably.

Block after block I try to convince myself that I can do it, that it's no big deal, such a small sacrifice to help a friend in need, that it would hardly cost me anything, and block after block the idea of showing up at City Hall with Yuri turns my stomach. All of my instincts are rebelling against taking such an action. But block after block, the voice pursues me, inexorably. It lives in my chest, pressing so hard I can hardly breathe. *You're selfish. Tu es la seule, toi. You are the only one. You have to think of others, those who are needy, who haven't had your privileged life. You are the only one who can do it.* I see my mother selling encyclopedias door

197

to door to raise money for the French Communist Party, I see her mounting her bicycle to follow the pilgrims' road to Saint-Jacques de Compostelle all by herself one summer when I was seventeen. I see her at dinner with my grandparents, her eyes burning with rage, with the same mad glow which lit up Yuri's eyes a couple of weeks ago, pounding on the table: "Hypocrite bastards, you're only thinking about yourselves, of your privileges."

Now is my chance to live up to her expectations.

I have asked Yuri to come over the following Saturday, when Lulu is at David's. He arrives carrying a bunch of Mr. Bean videos. He is a big fan. He pops *Merry Christmas Mr. Bean*, the one in which Mr. Bean, stuffing a monster turkey, sticks his head in its butt looking for his watch that fell in it, and then walks around with the bird on his head, frantically trying to pull it out. When his girlfriend shows up, he hides in the kitchen and through the door she asks, "Do you have the turkey on, dear?"

Yuri doubles over, in stitches.

After the video I make tea and we sit at the kitchen table. He takes out his keys and cell phone and sets them next to him as if he were expecting an urgent phone call.

"I am thinking of buying a little house upstate," I say, pouring the hot water into the teapot. "It was too scary to be trapped here during the attack."

"You have enough money to buy house?"

"I just sold my mother's place in the South of France."

His face lights up. "Really?"

I take cheese out of the fridge and lay it on a plate. He helps himself to a slice.

"So . . . ," he starts slowly, stirring sugar into his tea.

198

"What did you want to see me about?"

"I talked to a lawyer."

"You did?" His eyes open wide with astonishment and hope.

My heart sinks, remembering my dream of being locked in a room with a German shepherd guarding the door.

"So?"

I take a sip of tea to buy some time.

"It's not a good idea. You should forget about it."

He freezes, his spoon suspended in midair.

"Is what the lawyer said?"

"It's not what she said."

He drops the spoon and picks up his keys and waves them back and forth between us with an air of menace.

"You're playing with me. Like a puppet. One day yes, one day no. Like this. You're manipulating me."

"No."

"No what?

"It's no. I won't do it. I won't marry you. I've talked to the lawyer and thought about it and my *decision* is I won't do it."

A heavy silence, which he breaks with an explosion of rage.

"That's your decision?" He emphasizes the word with forced sarcasm. He cups his keys into his palm, grabs his phone and gets up, toppling the chair under him, and leaves without a word. A huge sense of relief floods my chest. He's gone. It's over. It wasn't so hard, really. All I had to do was say no. I feel light headed with relief, and ravenous.

# 5

October. Yuri calls me to apologize a few days later. My whole body stiffens at the sound of his voice. He continues cheerfully: he had no right to get so angry with me. Sometimes frustration is just too much and he loses it. Forget about marriage. He'll find another way. But he wants to keep seeing me. Could I come over for weekend and bring back videos?

As if nothing had happened. I let it sink for a beat.

The fog has descended again. My mind incoherently babbles on with some weak justification: one last time. One last time the Holland Tunnel, the Turnpike, the Jersey shore in the fall, the tearing wail of the seagulls, the metallic sea of lead, one last time my Saab parked by his van, the yellow leaves crushed under our feet in his desolate yard, one last time his gloomy little apartment. One last time and we'll break up for good.

On the Garden State, pulled by the same magnet that has drawn me to Yuri since the beginning, all joy and energy drained out of me, I drive as if I were simply submitting to my pre-ordained rendezvous with fate. All I want is to get the trip over with as soon as possible.

As ever, he comes out in the yard when he hears my car. But as soon as I tell him I have to go back to Manhattan the next day, he turns testy.

"So you just came here to eat and have sex and then you'll leave tomorrow morning?"

Ignoring his comment I place the Mr. Bean videos, a loaf of black, German bread and a piece of goat cheese on the counter.

"I brought you these."

"Why you have to tell me what you brought? So I notice how generous you are?"

I don't know what to say. He's just looking to start a fight. Any comment from me will only fuel his rage. He's already begun to prepare dinner—fried eggs, onions, green peppers—in the cast iron skillet I have given him. I am not hungry at all, but I set the table with the non-matching plates and the horn-handled vintage silverware, the ones he thinks of as "old and crappy," while he mutters that I only give him old stuff, "crap," leftovers. "Like you. I got your husband's leftovers. I never knew you when you were twenty-one."

How could I have let myself get trapped in his narrow, angry, abusive, sick mind? A year earlier, I'd like to think—although perhaps I am fooling myself—I would have walked out and driven right back to New York. But I have lost all willpower. I will spend the night and go back tomorrow. And then that will be the end. How foolish of me to think we could still see each other once the question of marriage had been put aside. We finish eating in silence and I gather the plates and wash them.

"In and out. You're always in and out," Yuri explodes

as I set the water up to heat on the stove. "I want a woman who's with me. A woman who cooks and shares a house with me. You don't want man. You don't need man. You just want sex. Why can't you be *hoooonest*? If you don't want to marry me you're only seeing me for sex. You're selfish and you don't love me."

The water is boiling. I pour it over the tea in the teapot and set the mugs on the coffee table.

"We said we wouldn't talk about that." I try to keep my voice calm and even.

I sit down on the Louis XV couch and fold one leg over the other. He points to my black and white hound's-tooth pants, the same ones I wore to go to his lawyer's.

"Why did you wear those pants?"

I shrug. "I like them."

"You're lying. Why did you wear them?"

All of a sudden the air is charged with menace. His steel-gray eyes are hard, his mouth tight, his back rigid.

I look at him without answering. His eyes remain fierce.

"Why can't you be *hoooonest*?"

It's at this moment that I feel danger.

My backpack is leaning against the couch, three steps away from me, my car parked in the yard. Manhattan is only two and a half hours away. And yet I don't get up. A force of inertia is keeping me glued to the couch. I must already know that I am his captive. Perhaps noticing a slight, unconscious movement toward my backpack, Yuri picks it up and holds it like a war trophy, pointing to the triangular Prada label on its flap.

"That cost $800." His voice snaps as if I had bought

the bag with his own, hard-won cash. Besides, how does he know that? Has he been reading Vogue again?

"It doesn't. More like $400. Anyway, I bought it in a thrift shop and only paid a hundred bucks for it," I protest, even though no justification is called for. Already, he's laid out the rules of the game. I have naively put myself at his mercy by refusing to marry him and not breaking up with him right then and there, and on top of that walking right into his lair. He dangles the backpack like he dangled the keys the other day, taunting me. Who knows if he's planned this or if holding the backpack gives him the idea? He must remember that, after he had thrown the jar of detergent against the wall, I had sneaked out while he was sleeping. He rummages in the bag, pulls the cord loose.

"Where are your keys? Give me your keys."

Adrenaline pumps in my heart. He opens the two outside pockets one after the other. In the second one he finds the keys and brandishes them. I don't try to grab them from him. I am mesmerized, paralyzed with fear. He is twice bigger than me. With one swipe of his hand, he'd throw me to the ground. I know no karate moves, I have taken no self-defense classes. I only have my wits, what's left of them. I was dumb enough to come here today. I try to hide my fear by playing it cool, as if he were a schoolboy playing a prank on me.

"You'll have to give them back to me. I need to leave early tomorrow."

He disappears into the bathroom, then into the bedroom. He moves powerfully, his body almost as tall and wide as the doorways. When he comes back my keys are not in his hands anymore.

"*If* you leave."

I sit back on the couch, forcing myself to calm down. He sits next to me, looking satisfied. He's easily won Round One. To ease the atmosphere, I suggest we watch the Christmas video. One more time, Mr. Bean is running around with the turkey stuck on his head. Behind the door, the fiancée asks, "Do you have the turkey on, dear?"

Yuri laughs, on cue.

"What are you going to do with the money you'll get from your mother's inheritance?" he asks out of the blue. "You still want to buy a house upstate?"

I freeze. So that's what he wanted to talk about.

"I don't know."

"I saw that there are cheap houses around Millville."

I tense up and say nothing.

"Landlord's mother is sick and he might want her to come live here. I don't have a lease. He can kick me out anytime. You could buy house upstate and I can live there. I'd pay you rent. Help you pay mortgage."

So he has it all figured out. He thought he would make me an offer that I couldn't refuse. A wave of anger rises in me at his naive presumption. The idea that I would buy a house upstate where Yuri would live is so far from anything I would ever do. He is right. I only wanted him as a lover. Not as a man in my life. I try to keep the pretense of a normal conversation.

"I don't know what I am going to do with the money. There's not much anyway. It's not a good time to bring francs to the States. The dollar is too strong. I should wait until they convert to the Euro. Or else I might buy a studio in Paris."

Mr. Bean is now offering a picture to his fiancée instead of the diamond ring she was dreaming of. She looks devastated.

"What about me?" His voice bellows, covering the video sound track. "I need house to open showroom. I am sick of being on the road all the time."

"I don't know. I can't tell you what to do."

What has he heard in my voice? That I'll never help him with his dream? That it's finally over? That he's played all his cards and there's only one option left?

He stands up, takes one step toward me and hits me on the back of the head, just behind the ear, maybe because it doesn't leave any mark there. Hard. One side. My eyes black out for a second. The other side. I fall on the couch, then sit back up, my heart pounding. Mr. Bean is now alone in his apartment, listening to the kids singing Christmas carols to his next door neighbor. His fiancée has run off, outraged at not getting her diamond ring.

Yuri is towering over me again.

"You said you'd buy house."

"It's a possibility. I don't know."

"How much did you get for your mother's place?"

I am loath to give him any explanation of my finances, but I don't want to oppose him head-on and provoke him.

"I don't know how much I'll end up with. Depends on the inheritance tax."

"Inheritance tax? Another capitalist dirty trick!"

He's at me again, his two hands around my neck, dragging me off the couch, choking me, his whole body, the 185 lbs of him, weighing down on me. Then, just as abruptly, he lets go of me.

"Don't," I say, uselessly. "Don't touch me."

The kettle whistles. He goes to the kitchen to make more tea. I disappear into the bathroom, which is adjacent to the living room, and close the door in case he is tempted to throw boiling water at me. It makes me feel safer, which is ridiculous since the door doesn't lock, but I am grasping at straws. I do a quick survey in case he's hidden my keys there, but I see nothing.

"*Chai? Budish?*" He calls through the door.

I come out and sit back on the couch to drink the tea. I talk to myself: don't antagonize. Keep things fluid and calm. Try to control the situation until his rage and his paranoia subside. Try to find an opening. He's your jailer and you are his hostage. You must outsmart him. It will take you the whole night, at least until he falls asleep. Be prepared to wait. Considering the difference between your weight and muscular abilities, that is your only way out: put the Giant to sleep, look for the keys, and escape behind his back.

"You're not saying anything?" he says.

"I am tired. Don't you want to sleep? Let's go to bed."

That was the wrong thing to say. He jumps up again and drags me off the couch on my knees all the way to the center of the room and circles my neck again with his hands.

"You're not Jew, are you? You didn't lie to me when you said you were not Jew?"

He pushes both his thumbs into my throat until I choke.

"Are you Jew?"

The pressure of his thumbs is suffocating.

"*Maman,*" I talk to her silently. "*Maman,* I took an insane risk. Please help me survive this. Protect me from up there, wherever you are."

"Are you Jew?"

In a flash, the poor communist I must save from deportation has turned into an S.S. about to send me to the gas chamber. With his blond buzz cut and his pale eyes, Yuri the Nazi has come back. Or is he Yuri the Soviet sweeping through Germany in a drunk, raping-and-slaying rampage?

"Are you?"

I shake my head no. He releases the pressure of his thumbs a little to allow me to speak. With horror I realize I am the kind of person who would denounce all her family at the first hint of torture. A traitor.

"Swear."

"I swear. I am not a Jew."

He hits me again, same place, behind the ear. And then above my temple, in my hair.

Before my scream has a chance to explode, his hand's on my mouth. With his other hand he grabs a bandanna that was lying on the desk and stuffs it into my mouth.

"If you make noise, if landlord hears anything, I kill you. If you try to call cops, I kill you."

He places his thumbs on my throat again, like he's done before, and presses hard.

I shake my head and try to get the gag out of my mouth. He pushes it back in with his fist.

"You swear?"

I nod forcefully. He drops the pressure on my mouth and throat and I cough out the bandanna.

"You swear?"

"Yes."

"I kill you."

We are both speaking in forced whispers. He pulls me up to my feet, pushes me into his big leather chair and looks at me with disdain. His eyelids suddenly drop.

"I'm going to bed. Don't even try to call cops or look for keys because I'll hear you. I'll hear you and I'll kill you. Come with me."

I follow him and lie down on the bed.

"Get undressed."

I get undressed except for my panties and my tank top. It takes him a long time to fall asleep. Every time I make a move, he senses it and seizes my wrist or mumbles something. It's only when the birds start to chirp and a pale light washes away the night, that sleep overtakes him. He snores lightly on his back. This is the moment I've been waiting for. I slip off the bed and search around the apartment for my keys. I go through the pockets of his jeans and his sweatshirt, run my hands on the shelf in his closet. Nothing. I open his desk drawer. Nothing. I look on top of the bathroom cabinet. Nothing. I pull on my pants, pick up my backpack and tiptoe outside to try to find a way out. My car is there, bright red and glistening with rain. I glance at it longingly. A festoon of raindrops splashes the windshield. I take out my cell phone. Six fifteen. I hesitate to call 911. What if he hears me?

Shit. He is at the door.

"What are you doing?"

"Nothing."

"Were you calling cops?"

"No. I . . . I just wanted to see what time it was."

"Outside?" His voice is sarcastic.

"I couldn't sleep."

He shakes his head suspiciously.

"Come back in."

I try to create a diversion. "How about breakfast?"

Once again he boils the water for tea. I take the German bread and the goat cheese out. The silence in the kitchen is suffocating. Before, alcohol was taking the edge off his rage. Now it's raw, smoldering again, although not as intense as during the night. We sit down wearily. I need to keep soothing him until a new opening occurs. After we finish breakfast, I propose to take a walk. I'd be safer outside than alone with him in his apartment.

We cross the road and walk in silence for a while following the tracks of a railroad I never knew was there. He walks one step ahead of me, his whole body alert, his back and shoulders rigid. If I tried to lose myself in the woods, he would catch me in a second. Wild reeds grow between the tracks. As we walk deeper into the forest, the tracks seem to be abandoned or little used, and the woods become bleaker, the fall leaves already fading and littering the soil. It's a subtle shift, like the setting of a dream seamlessly melting into a nightmare. After a few minutes, a sensation of cold penetrates me, even though streaks of sunlight sweep across the tracks.

"I think we should go back."

He turns around to face me and immediately picks up on my fear.

"Why?"

"I'd rather walk along the road. It's livelier."

"I like it here."

"It's strange, I never knew about those tracks."

We walk in silence for a while. Then he stops and points at the woods.

"You see those trees?

"Yes."

"If you died nobody would find you. If you were buried here."

My heart leaps up in panic.

He stands tall, his chin up, his eyes lost in the distance, his legs apart.

"Mother died younger than you are now. You deserve to die."

I try to calm the beatings of my heart.

"I'm sorry your mother died so young."

"Your being sorry doesn't change anything." His voice is thunderous. Any fatigue left over from the short night is swept away. His fury is revived afresh. His body stiffens, his eyes look fierce.

"Your death will make up for hers."

Is that what a murderer looks like? Rigid, his features frozen? He could have killed me during the night. With just a little more pressure from his thumbs. He could strangle me now. Snap my neck in two with his enormous hands. I would struggle like I did last night, but he wouldn't worry about my screams. Nobody would hear me.

On the side of the tracks the woods lie in shadows. The leaves are already decomposing. He would be methodical in digging the grave. There must be a shovel somewhere in his van or in the garage. The soil, moist from last night's rain, would give in easily. He would pick me up and carry me like a cloth doll. In the wintertime the snow would cover the tracks, cover the undergrowth, like it covered his mother's body. He's right, nobody would come and look for me. Nobody knows I am here. Not any of my friends. Not Ludivine. Lulu! Oh Lulu! My God, Lulu! What would happen to her when she found out her mother was dead and how she was killed? For what? To finally be worthy of my mother's ideals? To punish myself for her death? Because I didn't have the courage to stand up to Yuri and break up with him last week? Because I was too naive, too reckless to see this coming?

He holds me in his cold gaze, taking his time.

Has he planned this? Would he kill in cold blood?

There's the slightest shift in his posture, an almost imperceptible slackening of his muscles, as though he was too tired to hold the tension.

"I want you to go to Moscow," he says. "I want you to put flowers on mother's grave for me. Since I am trapped here and can't leave country. White lilies."

"OK." I take a quick breath, sensing an opening. "I will." I take a tentative step in the direction we came from, to test him.

"Wait!"

I turn around. He's still standing the same way, his legs apart, his eyes staring fixedly in the distance.

"Let's go home." I coax him gently.

He follows me. We walk behind each other along the tracks, me in front this time. I try to keep my pace even. The backyard is still quiet when we get back to the house. He goes straight to the bedroom and stretches on the bed. His fury is spent.

"Come lie down with me."

"I have to go back soon." I speak in a very soft voice, as in a dream, so as not to wake up the Giant. "I'll need my keys back."

He stares at me for a moment. His eyes have lost their furious glow. They look hazy as if they had lost the power to see. He runs his hand under the mattress and pulls my keys out, showing them to me in his half-cupped hand, then closing his fingers on them.

"Promise you'll lie down with me for a while first."

I hold my breath. "OK."

He hands me the keys and I put them in my backpack and go back to the bedroom. He's already under the sleeping bag, still dressed. The mask of his face has loosened, softening the brutal carnality of his forehead, of his long, thin lips. I lie down next to him. After a while he unzips my pants, slips on top of me and enters me. He moves inside of me with a rare gentleness and comes almost right away. A wave of sadness and pity washes over me.

"I can't believe I did what I did," he mumbles. "What I did to you. . . ."

I roll over to the side, gently slipping off the bed.

"Don't." His hand brushes the back of my arm to hold me back but it's already dissolving into sleep.

I touch his forehead with my fingers and leave the room. I pick up my backpack and let myself out and put my boots on outside. It's five minutes after ten.

The Saab starts up right away. I pull around the driveway, but just when I am about to turn into the road, he appears in my side mirror. My heart bangs in my chest but there's a car coming on the other side, blocking me from moving forward. Already he's leaning at the passenger window, which I had pressed open to air the humidity.

"You're leaving," he says.

"Yes." My breath skips a beat. My hand is on the gearshift, my left foot on the clutch, my right foot on the gas pedal.

"You're leaving for good."

I say nothing.

"I'll never see you again."

His face is creased with sleep. Along his right temple the sheet has left a pink line, almost like a fading scar. I slowly let the clutch go as I give a little gas and ease into first gear. The car moves just a notch but his arms are still leaning at the window, not letting it go.

I press the gas pedal and release the clutch. The car jumps.

"*Do zvidannya*," I say.

He lifts his arms off the window and steps aside.

I press on the gas. I make the left turn on the road without looking into the rearview mirror and speed towards the highway. The Saab takes the turns with the same ease it took them going down. The phone rings. I turn it off. It's really over this time. The spell is broken. There's no elation, barely a hint of relief, only a deep sadness. I turn off the stereo and drive in silence. Along the Garden State the trees are flaming orange and red, a sumptuous tapestry of fall foliage. The sky is piercing blue. Autumn in the American Northeast, lush, abundant, glorious. Each turn of the wheels takes me further away from Yuri's desolate little pad, from his desperate machinations, from his broken dreams. The silence is profound. Manhattan comes at me full speed ahead, my life sketched in crystal-clear strokes: Lulu at school, the laptop on my desk, the Indochina novel that will soon be finished, the kitchen flooded with light in which I will cook dinner. The frenzy that has fueled me since David left has finally run its course, smashed smack into a wall.

The fear came later. The few days spent at Alba's with Lulu in case Yuri got the idea to hold siege at my front door, the hasty arrangements to protect us. Changing my cell phone number. Calling the matrimonial lawyer and asking her to write a threatening letter to Yuri so that he lays off me or else—finally resorting to the same tactic Tasha had used. Booking a plane ticket to go to France to empty out my mother's apartment and extending my stay for a few weeks until things cooled off, while Lulu stayed at her dad's. The fear gripping me whenever I saw a white Lincoln or a blue van on my block. The fear when someone called and I didn't recognize the number, or when someone called and hung up.

Yuri did call me a year later, and then several times after that. Each time I hung up in panic as soon as I heard his voice, and walked to my front windows to check whether his car was parked at the curb. One day, three or four years later, he called again and I didn't hang up on him. We talked and he apologized. He said he didn't know what got into him, that what he did was unforgivable. Once he called me from Moscow, and then again from the States—he had miraculously gotten his green card, I didn't try to find out how. He wanted to meet me. I refused. Over the years, the phone calls have become less and less frequent, and my fear has eased. It's an old story, now, for both of us. Soon ten years will have passed. We've both grown older. In his last phone call he told me he was losing his hair and he had backaches from being on the road all the time. I didn't tell him that I had more white hair – although I dye it. I didn't tell him either that I had fallen in love with another Russian man. Eventually the man I had fallen in love with vanished from my life. That too, now, is beginning to feel like an old story. The river of time never stops.

**RAW**MEASH

26536492R00137

Made in the USA
Middletown, DE
02 December 2015